THE BACHELORETTE RESCUE

TEXAS HOTLINE SERIES, BOOK #6

JO GRAFFORD

Second Edition. This book was previously part of the Disaster City Search and Rescue Series. It has since been revised and recovered to be included in the Texas Hotline Series.

Cover Design by Jo Grafford

ISBN: 978-1-63907-006-0

ACKNOWLEDGMENTS

Thank you to my editor, Cathleen Weaver, and to my amazing beta readers, Mahasani and Debbie Turner. I also want to give a shout-out to my Cuppa Jo Readers on Facebook for reading and loving my books!

GET A FREE BOOK!

Join my mailing list to be the first to know about new releases, freebies, special discounts, and Bonus Content. Plus, you get a FREE sweet romance book for signing up!

https://BookHip.com/JNNHTK

ABOUT THIS SERIES

Welcome to the Texas Hotline, a team of search and rescue experts — police officers, firefighters, expert divers, and more. In an emergency, your sweet and swoon-worthy rescuer is only a phone call away.

CHAPTER 1: IMAGINARY KISS

REESE

Most people assumed Reese Summerville was a thrill-seeker like her sailing champion mother had been. Nothing could be further from the truth, though. *Shoot!* At the age of twenty-five, she still closed her eyes and held her nose when jumping into the deep end of the pool. However, being labeled a thrill-seeker certainly sounded better than what really motivated her — guilt.

Tossing her snow shoes into the back seat of her silver Land Rover, Reese slammed the door shut. Three years after the tragic loss of her mother, guilt was what continued to drive her. It was the sole reason she'd poured her entire inheritance into the start-up of her own survivalist reality show, Max West Adventures — a show whose ratings had quickly rocketed to the top of the charts. A show that currently had a list of candidates a mile long waiting for her next round of tryouts...

"Yo, Reese! Over here!" an unfamiliar male voice shouted in an overly familiar tone.

Stinking reporters! Knowing the man was merely trying to get a good angle on an unauthorized head-shot of her, Reese kept her face carefully averted from his flashing camera bulb. She yanked open the passenger door and leaped inside.

"Let's get out of here," she snarled to the head of her film crew.

"Whoa there, cowgirl!" Garek Borden started the ignition in his usual unhurried manner and rolled at a snail's pace across the crowded parking lot. "Who rained on your rodeo?" He fiddled with a button to adjust his side-view mirror, presumably to get a better look at the equipment trailer they were towing.

"Just drive," Reese instructed tiredly. She pulled her Stetson lower over her forehead, hoping to discourage anyone who might have a zoom lens trained on the tinted windows of her SUV.

"Okay." Garek's shrug made his broad shoulders flex beneath his red and white plaid shirt — not that she had any business noticing stuff like that. "Hate passing up the opportunity for free publicity, though," he continued. "For all we know, that joker back there could have hundreds of thousands of social media followers."

She peeked out from beneath her beige felt hat brim to scowl at him. "Or he might just be some creep trying to make a buck by throwing my face on his black market merch." Which would totally cannibalize the sales of the legally licensed merchandise featured in her online store. *Gosh!* Reese was still wrapping her brain around the fact that her survivalist show had become popular enough to start selling stuff like t-shirts, hoodies, and autographed posters.

Garek shook his dark head sadly at her. "How a nervous Nellie like you ended up becoming the owner of a survivalist show is beyond me."

"I'm not nervous, just cautious," she snapped.

"Tomato, to-mah-to," he scoffed.

"And you know the reason why."

"Yeah." To her surprise, he reached across the gray leather console to take her hand. "I do."

There was no mistaking the sympathy in his voice, which made her even more irritable than she already was. She wasn't looking for his sympathy or anyone else's. The possessive way his large hand enveloped hers was even more concerning. She blew out a breath as she stared at their joined hands — his long, dark fingers laced through her more delicate, much lighter ones.

"What are you doing, Garek?" *Correction. What are we doing?*

"What does it look like, sugar?"

"I have eyes," she sighed, wondering why the southern endearments he always used on her felt like they were charged with more emotion than usual today. Either that, or her imagination was running in overdrive. "I guess what I'm really asking is why?"

She and Garek were close, almost like family. They'd grown up next door to each other — sharing everything from PB&J sandwiches to their deepest, most heartfelt secrets. She didn't want that to change. Ever. Lately, however, she'd become worried that his feelings for her were going through some sort of metamorphosis. Already, their relationship felt different from the way it had even a month ago. It was a problem she didn't have an answer for, though she was pretty sure it was something they would have to deal with soon.

"Relax. I'm holding your hand because you're upset, and it's the only thing I can do about it while I'm driving."

It was an innocent-sounding excuse, one she wasn't buying. "I'm not upset."

His fingers momentarily tightened over hers. "Lying to me has never been one of your strengths, so why bother?"

She glanced worriedly again at their joined hands. "I just don't want things to get weird between us, okay?"

His black brows shot comically upward. "We've known each other our entire lives. Trust me, babe,

I've already witnessed most of your weirdest moments."

Darling, sugar, babe... Nope. She wasn't simply imagining things. He really was pouring on the charm this morning. But why? She gently tugged her hand away from his. "Thanks, I think."

"You're welcome." He didn't look the least perturbed by her withdrawal. Placing his hand back on the steering wheel, he started to whistle beneath his breath. "Fine. Since you refuse to hold my hand during our long, lonely drive," his voice was mocking, "how about we talk, instead?"

"About what?" She held her breath. *Please don't say it. Please don't say it.*

"Your feelings."

If they weren't rolling along the highway at full speed, she might've considered yanking open the door and jumping from the vehicle. Catching her lower lip between her teeth, she muttered, "What are you talking about?" She wasn't in the mood to discuss her feelings, so there was no way she was going to make this conversation easy on him.

"About the worst night of your life. The one that haunts you twenty-four seven, though we never seem to get around to talking about it."

Right. Those feelings. With a long, whooshy exhale, she wilted against the leather seat, no longer trying to hide her face from view. Garek had probably already put enough distance between them and that annoying reporter.

"Talk to me, Reese." Garek's voice turned grave. "It's time. We've put this off long enough."

She squeezed her eyelids shut. "I don't want to talk about it." *Much less think about it.*

"I know you don't, darling, but you need to."

"I can't. Please don't make an issue out of it. You're supposed to be my best—"

"Don't bother playing the friend card with me," he interrupted. "This conversation is long overdue, and you know it. What happened that night has been eating you alive for three straight years. I've been patient, hoping time would heal you, but it hasn't. The nightmares are back, aren't they?"

She cracked her eyelids open and squinted at him through a shaft of morning sunlight. "Why are you doing this to me?"

He was silent for a moment, opening his mouth as if he was about to say something, then shutting it. He finally started speaking again. "Because you're about to go on set in the middle of winter, which is not something we've done before. For the past three show seasons, we've headed for the tropics this time of year."

"Yeah, so?" She lifted her chin. Braving the winter elements on her survivalist show was a challenge she was looking forward to. So were her biggest fans.

They were all a-buzz about the upcoming opening episode that bazillions of bloggers and podcasters were already referring to as *the Christmas episode.*

"I've done my research. Heart Lake is known for its last-minute snowstorms, avalanches, and bear sightings during the winter months."

"Aw, are you scared?" Reese teased.

"More like concerned," he shot back. "For you. Like a good friend should be."

She chuckled. "Now who's playing the friend card?"

"Quit trying to distract me with your beautiful laugh. Answer the question already." He tipped his Stetson back to pin her with one of his inscrutable, uniquely Garek looks.

It sounded like he was in one of his dog-with-a-juicy-bone moods. Knowing he wouldn't be easily sidetracked, she caved. "Yes, the nightmares are back." Just thinking about them was giving her the start of a headache.

"Figured they were." His jaw tightened. "I have a solution, but you're not going to like it."

She waved a hand. "I don't like anything about this conversation, but lay it on me anyway. You know you want to." The sooner he got whatever was bothering him off his chest, the better for both of them.

"You need to quit blaming yourself for what happened. It's not your fault, Reese. None of it was your fault."

Her lips parted in shock. "How can you say that?" she demanded. A mixture of fury and puzzlement tightened her gut. Gosh, she adored Garek to pieces, but he'd finally gone too far.

"Because it's true," he growled between clenched teeth. "You didn't make your mother go on that final boat ride, any more than you conjured up the storm that blew her off course."

"Yes, but I should've been there." To Reese's dismay, tears stung the backs of her eyelids. She wasn't in the mood to cry. Crying never made her feel better — just all wrung out afterward. "My Mom invited me to go with her. Bet you didn't know that. After all those years of being on the road, she finally tried to include me in something, and I—"

"You had other commitments. I remember. Term ends, to be exact." He flicked on the left blinker to pass a lumbering dump truck on the two-lane highway.

"I probably could've rescheduled one of my term ends," she choked, "but I didn't even try. If only I'd given my mom a different answer to her invitation!"

"I'm selfishly glad you didn't." Garek's voice turned rough. "I'm afraid I'd have lost you, too."

"You don't know that." Her voice shook. "I might be cautious, but I'm no coward. I've always been the planner of the family. I would've brought along a compass, a radio, and a full supply of snacks..." She had to stop and clear her throat at the realization that she was mentally checking off the list of basic survival supplies she drilled into her show contestants. As the old saying went, hindsight was 20-20. The bald truth was that three years ago she wouldn't have been nearly as prepared for an outdoor emergency as she was today.

"She crashed into the rocks," Garek reminded in a low, terse voice. "Her supplies went down with the boat. Yours would have, too."

"Still," Reese's voice was thready, "there would have been two of us out there together. Two heads are better than one."

"Finally, something we can agree on," he noted gently. "That's why we're having this conversation. Two sets of shoulders are also better than one. It's about time you let me share the weight of that horrific night with you."

The tears Reese had been holding back finally broke loose. "I can't share it," she wailed. Her voice rose to a nearly hysterical pitch. "You aren't the one who had a huge argument with your mother right before her final sailing trip. You aren't the one who said things you can't ever take back." She swiped at the wetness on her face with both hands. "Oh, sheesh! This is what talking about it always does to me. I'm a complete wreck now. I hope you're happy."

She felt the SUV slow as Garek moved back into the right lane and feathered the brakes. Through blurry eyes, she watched him pull into the exit lane leading to the next rest stop.

He pulled into the semi-truck parking lot and coasted to a stop at the far edge of the lot. Silence settled between them.

With a muttered expulsion, he threw open the driver's door and jogged around to her side of the vehicle. He opened her door and stared at her for a moment.

"No, your unhappiness doesn't make me happy," he growled, gesturing for her to step out. "I can't believe you said that."

"Where are we going?" she quavered, hating herself a little for hurting his feelings like that.

"Not far," he promised. Reaching for her elbow, he towed her across the short strip of asphalt to the sidewalk.

She didn't offer any resistance as he led her across the grassy park-like area to a picnic table. She didn't even put up a fuss when he placed his hands on her slender waist and lifted her to sit on top of the table.

The brisk mountain breeze made her shiver and wrap her arms around her middle.

In response, Garek canted his broad shoulders sideways to block the worst brunt of the wind from her. "You're right. I didn't have a fight with your mom the night of the tragedy. I'm sorry that you did, but it still doesn't make her crash your fault."

"But she was so upset with me, Garek. Being in that frame of mind wouldn't have helped her steer out of any trouble she found herself in." Reese stopped and gulped for air as the old familiar guilt worked its way like poison through her gut.

"Mind if I ask what you were fighting about?" Folding his arms, Garek dipped his head to look her straight in the eyes.

Something inside her shuddered at the big-drink look he was giving her. There was no other way to describe it. Sometimes, Garek had a way of gazing all the way through her. It never failed to leave her heart feeling exposed.

She shook her head at him, too emotionally exhausted to dodge his question. He was never going to quit asking, so she might as well get it over with. "You," she said simply.

He leaned back a few inches without dropping her gaze. "Me?" He sounded so caught off guard that she chuckled despite her tears.

"The one and only Garek Borden," she affirmed ruefully.

"Okay. Not following you. I honestly don't remember doing anything to cause a fight between you and your mom."

"Of course you didn't." Without thinking, Reese reached out to give his folded arms a reassuring pat.

Without unfolding his arms, he clapped a hand over hers and held it there. "Still not following you."

"She, ah..." Not bothering to pull her hand away, Reese tipped her head up to the clouds and rolled her eyes. "What I'm about to say cannot get past the two of us, you hear?"

"I've never breathed a word about any of your secrets, darling, so spill."

Reese closed her eyes, feeling the heat rise to her cheeks. "Well, for one thing, my mom thought I was way overreacting about your decision to volunteer for the fire department."

"Interesting," he sounded mildly amused, "considering I don't recall you having any reaction to it whatsoever. I was pretty hacked about that at the time," he confessed. "I wouldn't have minded you at least acting like you cared about the risks I was taking."

"Actually, I was furious with you." She opened her eyes to meet his gaze again. "We were both in college. I didn't see any point in doing something so stupidly dangerous."

"Stupid, eh? Wow! You don't hold back." He snorted. "Sorry, darling, but I'm going to have to agree with your mother on this one. That was definitely an over-reaction from a woman who turned around and started her own survivalist reality show."

"You might have a point."

"You know I do." He smirked. "What's so bad about that? You worry about me, and I worry about you. Friends have a right to do that. I don't see any point in arguing with your mom about something like that."

Lord, give me strength. Reese glanced away. She'd come too far in the conversation to back out now. "She insisted the reason I was so upset about you joining the fire department was because you and I were more than friends." There. She'd finally said it. *Awkward!* But now Garek knew the truth about that night. Well, most of it. She risked another glance in his direction to gauge his reaction to what she'd said.

His expression was hard to read. "The mistake was understandable. You and I lived in each other's pockets back then."

We still do. She made a face at him. "I told her she was way wrong about us. Then she insisted on knowing if we'd ever kissed, and I sort of lost it after that." She blushed at the memory. One thing had led to another, and she had eventually accused her mother of trying to compensate for being an absent parent by butting her nose into things that didn't concern her. "I'm sad to say that the last thing I told her wasn't that I loved her. The last thing I said was that I was glad she was shipping off again, because being gone was the one thing she was good at." Tears blurred her vision at the memory.

Her mother had gotten the last word in, though. Sheree Summerville had finally admitted that Reese was right... about everything. In comparison, she'd allowed her career to push away the people she cared about the most. She was only trying to keep Reese from making the same mistake. Her exact words were, "Don't push Garek away, baby girl. He's the one regret you'll never recover from if you do."

Unfortunately, Sheree Summerville hadn't made it home. Reese would never get to apologize for the things she'd said out of anger, nor would she ever again get to tell her mother how much she loved her. Some things in life simply didn't come with a do-over button. She dropped her head in sheer misery.

Garek's warm fingers on her chin made her glance up again. "Thank you for finally telling me what happened."

"There was a little more to it than that, but you get the gist of it." She sniffled guiltily, knowing she'd withheld the most important part of their argument from him. "Now you know what an awful person I am."

He rolled his eyes. "I'm pretty sure you're not the first college kid who's ever had a disagreement with her mother."

"You have to admit it was a doozy of a last argument to have, though." Reese balled her fists in her lap. "I wish I could erase every single word of it and just tell her that I love her, instead."

He nodded. "She knew it. Trust me."

Reese blinked and swiped at more tears. "I try to tell myself that, but I didn't say it enough, Garek."

She and her mother had argued way too much during her college years. Her mother's temperament had undergone a drastic change during that time. She'd signed up for so many sailing competitions, it was as if she was trying to avoid begin a parent altogether. "And now I can't say it at all."

He reached over to lightly pinch her chin. "It was a waterspout that blew out of nowhere. It happened so fast that it never hit the forecast reports. I think you know way down deep inside that your being there wouldn't have changed a thing." His lips twisted. "If you'd have been on that boat, you likely wouldn't have made it back either. It would have actually cost two more lives — yours and mine." The burst of passion in his voice made her stare.

"Yours, huh?" She slapped his hand away from her chin in an attempt to restore a bit of lightness to their conversation. "You're so full of it. This isn't about you."

"Really?" His black brows rose again. "Because I seem to recall it all started with an argument about a kiss I never gave you."

Her eyes widened. "Seriously? That's all you got out of my soul-baring fest here?"

He nodded, looking smug. "I'd say our kiss that never happened is a pretty big part of it."

"You mean our kiss that's never going to happen," she taunted. Hopping down from the table, she faced him, fully expecting him to back up and give her more room to walk around him.

He didn't. "Never is a long time, darling. What about birthdays and holidays? You'd think they'd warrant at least a peck on the cheek now and then."

They stared each other down for a moment the way they had when they were kids. His gaze was narrowed in calculation on hers, which in no way distracted her from the way his tall frame towered protectively over her or how well his chest filled his button-up shirt. No doubt about it, Garek Borden was smoking hot in jeans and boots. He probably knew it, too.

She lifted her chin. "Okay, fine. Best friends might end up air kissing or something, but we're not...that is, I'm not..." She searched for the right word.

"Not my girlfriend?" He unfolded his arms to spread them. "Not interested in kissing me? Or afraid of what might happen if you do?"

She felt a fresh wave of red blossom on her cheeks. "All the above." *Omigosh!* She couldn't believe they were having such a crazy conversation.

The laughter disappeared from his gaze. It was replaced by something much warmer — so much warmer that it turned his eyes a melting shade of brown. "Haven't you at least wondered about what it would be like to kiss me?"

She gasped. "No! Of course not!"

"Really?" Though he sounded amazed, the twinkle returned to his eyes.

"No. Not even once!" She was suddenly anxious to end the conversation. It had taken a turn that she didn't quite know what to think of. "Why? Have you?"

At his slow grin, she held up a hand. "No, don't answer that. I don't want to know."

"Liar." He bent his head closer to croon the word directly in her ear.

Argh! She pushed around him, hoping he didn't see her smile.

"You'll probably think about it now," he called silkily after her.

"You're impossible," she muttered.

"You're welcome."

For what? She paused during her march away from him. "So, ah...I'm gonna visit the ladies' room before getting back in the car. That way, this ridiculous stop won't end up being a complete waste of my time." However, her heart felt much lighter than it had before he'd insisted on talking.

The truth was, Garek knew how to handle her no matter what kind of mood she happened to be in. He always had. It was the dangerous thing about having a best friend like him.

CHAPTER 2: MEETING THE COMPETITION

GAREK

Garek made a point of beating Reese back to the main sidewalk in front of the rest stop. He propped the toe of one cowboy boot on an empty park bench and leaned his forearm on his knee. Watching for her reappearance out of the corner of his eye, he scowled at his watch when she sauntered in his direction.

"Good grief!" He faked a glare as he straightened. "I was beginning to wonder if you were going to keep me waiting all afternoon." He shook his head in mock derision.

She swatted at his shoulder and kept walking. He held up his fists, assuming the stance of a boxer, and danced directly in her path. When she deliberately plowed into him, his heart pounded at her answering show of playfulness.

Man, but she was fun to tease! He gently clasped

her shoulders, reveling in her nearness while allowing his broad frame to absorb the biggest brunt of their impact.

Somehow her hands ended up splayed flat against his chest, a situation he didn't mind at all. She cocked her heart-shaped face at him, giving her long, blonde ponytail a sassy toss over one shoulder. She'd left her Stetson in the SUV, another detail he found noteworthy. It meant she trusted him to protect her from the paparazzi.

"I don't know why I even keep you around," she grumbled in a petulant voice. "You're nothing but trouble."

"I know why," he retorted without hesitation. "It's so I can do all the heavy lifting. You know... loading and hitching the trailer, driving, and unloading everything for you when we get there."

He liked the fact that she seemed in no hurry to move away from him. As she continued to stare up at him in cheeky consideration, he couldn't help thinking that she was within easy kissing distance. All he would have to do was lean a few inches closer to capture her mouth with his — her very sassy, very pouty, very enticing lips.

He intended to do exactly that someday, eyes wide open so he could watch her expressive baby blues go all soft and smoky with emotion...or at least that was how he imagined their first kiss would be.

She wrinkled her nose. "That sounds about right."

"Wow! Did you just give me a compliment?" He feigned surprise.

She shook her head, looking innocent. "I didn't hear one."

"Yeah." He waggled a finger in front of her nose. "I'm pretty sure you just slipped up and admitted I'm useful to have around." He shrugged. "In so many words."

She was so beautiful, standing there in front of him, that she made his heart ache. Since they were between shows, her face was free of makeup — exactly the way he liked it — and her windblown hair was practically begging him to smooth the stray wisps back. In lieu of a coat, she'd tossed an oversized gray sweatshirt over a hot pink tank top, which she'd paired with simple black leggings. It was what she called her sloppy look, though he couldn't have disagreed more. To him, she simply looked relaxed. And more touchable...

Without thinking, he dipped his head closer to hers. Her expression turned anxious, then accusing. "Please assure me you're not thinking about kissing me again," she squeaked. She gave his chest a quick shove.

"What? No way!" His gaze inevitably dropped to her mouth. "Wouldn't dream of it," he lied. "You're my boss."

"No, I'm not! I wish you'd quit saying that."

The vehemence in her voice surprised him. "Aren't you the woman who writes my paychecks?"

She wrinkled her nose at him. "Yes, but I include you in all the important stuff, all the big decisions, everything that affects our bottom line. That makes us more like partners."

Not officially, but okay. He liked where she was going with the conversation, even though he wasn't near finished teasing her. "Well, your business partner's thoughts about you are all business. Trust me."

"I don't," she shot back with a sassy tilt to her chin.

"Don't what?" he pretended to misunderstand.

"Trust you."

"Okay, now I'm wounded." He laid a hand over his heart. "Right here."

Her eyes twinkled merrily back at him. "I'll make it up to you."

"Okay, I'll bite. How?"

To his intense disappointment, she stepped around him to walk back to the Land Rover. "I'm considering giving you an extra two or three minutes to unload the trailer after we arrive on set."

Says the boss to her underling. "Your generosity knows no bounds." He stared after her, not bothering to hide his sarcasm, and was immediately distracted by the feminine sway to her steps.

By the time he realized he was staring like an

idiot, he had to jog to catch up to her. "Want a leg up?" he asked as they reached the passenger door of her SUV.

Instead of smiling at his comparison of her vehicle to a horse, she held out a hand. "No, I want the keys. It's my turn to drive, if for no other reason than to shoot holes in your claim that you're always stuck doing all the driving."

"No can do, boss lady." He lowered her hand back to her side, though he didn't immediately let it go. Interestingly enough, she didn't pull it away either. "Only a few minutes ago, you admitted you haven't been sleeping well. Probably best for me to keep driving while you try to catch some Z's."

Her cheeks turned a delightful shade of irritated. "I am not going to snooze away this entire trip. I'd never hear the last of your complaining if I did."

She didn't seem to notice that they were still holding hands. "Then you'll just have to live with my complaining." He used their joined hands to tug her closer so he could speak directly into her ear. "Oh, and try not to snore too loud. I'm listening to a new soundtrack."

She drew back in outrage. "I do *not* snore, Garek Borden!"

"How would you know?" He waggled his brows at her. "Seeing as how you're asleep when—"

"I don't snore," she snapped again.

It was true. She didn't, but he was enjoying

getting a rise out of her on the topic. "Not sure what you're so worried about." He reached over to lightly tap her nose. "Like I said earlier, all of your secrets are safe with me, sugar."

She yanked open the passenger door and flounced into her seat. "You know what? I'm too tired to keep arguing. But if I could, I'd seriously snore loud enough to drown out your entire stinking soundtrack."

"Impressive." Garek curled his upper lip at her. "Then again, I already knew you're a woman of many talents." He was relieved that she'd caved on the driving issue without him having to wrestle her into the passenger seat. He wished she was his to lean in and kiss. Instead, he shut her door for her and walked around to the driver's side.

As they buckled their seatbelts, she frowned over at him. "Do you feel unsafe when I drive?" Her voice was hesitant, alerting him to the fact that she was genuinely worried about it.

"No. I was just kidding about the snoring. I thought you knew that." He always messed with her when he was trying to cover the fact that he was looking out for her. "But we can't afford any mistakes. We've got a big season coming up, which means we all need to stay on top of our game. Right now that means yielding the keys to your lowly camera guy."

"Lowly?" She sniffed. "Did you seriously just call yourself lowly?"

"Yes, ma'am." He spoke in his humblest voice and tipped his hat at her. Then he started the ignition.

"As if!" Chuckling, she waved her hands to take in the surrounding cab. "There's no vehicle big enough to contain all of your cockiness."

"Thanks." He watched out of the corner of his eye as she settled her head back against the seat and closed her eyes.

"It wasn't a compliment," she murmured, still chuckling as she reclined her seat a few inches.

"Sure, it was. You wouldn't be the first person to mistake cockiness for confidence." As they rolled from the parking lot, he casually reached over to rest a hand on the back of her seat.

In the same moment, she turned her face toward him, eyes still closed, to snuggle against the seat cushion. Her movements caused the pad of his thumb to brush against her cheek.

Instead of pulling back, she reached up and lightly caressed his thumb before dropping her hand back in her lap. "You're both of those things," she murmured, still not opening her eyes. "Cocky and confident. Like I said before, you're a lot more than a cameraman to me."

He turned onto the entrance to the highway,

wondering what she meant by that. However, her slender frame had grown still. She was asleep.

He was glad to see she was resting. Unfortunately, it meant he would get to spend the next couple of hours wondering just how much more than a cameraman he was to her. Back in college, he'd convinced himself they were finally heading in the direction of becoming more than friends. However, her mother's death had all too effectively slapped the pause button on that.

Instead of dating Reese, he'd spent the last three years watching her go through a thousand stages of grieving. Helping her start her own survivalist reality show had been a part of that process. It was like she was trying to save her mother again and again. Only during the last few months had he felt like the two of them were finally working their way back to some semblance of normal. And now he was trying to figure out when was the best time to finally move their relationship to the next level. It was the question of the century.

With a long-suffering exhale, Garek leaned toward the dashboard to switch on the new movie soundtrack he'd purchased a few days ago. He kept the volume low — too low to hear the words, but loud enough to provide a background of white noise that would hopefully help Reese sleep. It had always been this way between them. He was forever making sacrifices to further her happiness, career, and success. And he was glad to do it. He had it that bad for her.

Yeah, I'm a fool for you, baby. Everyone but her seemed to know it, including the owner of Dallas PM Sports Channel, who'd offered him a camera crew position last week that easily would've paved his way into the big networks. Even his own mother thought he was a fool to pass it up.

Some girls are like the wind, she'd said. *Chase Reese Summerville all you want, sweetheart, but you're never gonna catch her. Never gonna keep her.*

But his mom hadn't heard Reese's last words before falling asleep. *You're a lot more than a cameraman to me.* Moments like that were what fueled his biggest hopes and dreams in her direction — that someday he would be a *lot* more to her than her lowly cameraman.

But for now, he was content to be a fool, *her* fool, the man passing up a big career opportunity to follow her to some remote mountain town called Heart Lake. He still wasn't clear on why she'd chosen this particular location for their next big television shoot, but he trusted her business instincts. She was the heart and soul of Max West Adventures; he was just the muscle. For now.

One topic he was crystal clear on was the fact that she wanted the next episode they filmed together to be brimming with Christmas cheer, something he was going to do everything in his power to make happen. Bring on the holly, tinsel, and lights, baby!

———————

REESE SLEPT SO SOUNDLY through the final few hours of their drive to Heart Lake that Garek passed his hand beneath her nose a few times to make sure she was still breathing. As he turned onto the main highway leading to the downtown area, he held his hand in front of her face again.

"I'd suggest you remove your paw before I take a bite out of it," she warned in a sleepy voice.

"You're finally awake." He grinned in her direction. "I was beginning to wonder if you were going to hibernate for the rest of the winter."

Ignoring his comment, she stretched and sat up. "Gosh, I'm famished!"

"*You're* famished?" he scoffed. "I'm the one who's spent the last several hours working up an appetite over here."

"Hey, I offered," she reminded airily. "Couldn't get you to uncurl your claws from the keys."

Though he smirked at her words, he merely pointed out the window.

Her gaze followed his arm, and what she saw made her gasp. "Oh, Garek! We're here." Her squeal of delight was laced with anticipation. "The lake, the mountains," she sighed. "It's just like I remembered."

He agreed that Heart Lake was a stunning slice of countryside. The enormous lake that the town was named after rested like a mammoth ice crystal in the center of town. The highway twisted in a half-circle around it and continued on toward the white-capped mountains in the distance. Snow-drenched barns and houses were perched around the lake's frozen edges. A few skaters zipped their way across the ice, sunlight glinting from the blades beneath their feet.

However, the beauty of the scene stretching before them didn't erase the burning questions Garek still had about the trip as a whole. "I'll admit, I was surprised when you announced you were filming an entire season of your show here."

"We were invited," she said simply.

"Right. By a distant uncle you never mentioned before now." He curled his upper lip, hoping she'd elaborate on her relationship with this elusive corner of her family.

Either she didn't pick up on his hint, or she was ignoring it. "He went to a lot of trouble to make the arrangements for us to come here," she reminded. "He even enlisted his nephew's help in securing all the appropriate permissions to use the arena and stuff. How could I say no?"

Nephew? It was the first time Reese had mentioned a cousin was in the picture. "I'm glad you didn't say no. Now that I see the lake and mountains for myself, I understand why you jumped on the opportunity."

"That's not the only reason." She finally glanced over at him, looking a little nervous.

"Oh?" His gut had been telling him there was more to the story. Looked like he was right.

"I'll be handling some personal business during this trip, something I probably should have mentioned before."

He couldn't have been more mystified. "I'm listening." If his memory served him, she and her mom had taken a few vacations in this town back when they were in high school. However, he couldn't recall anything out of the ordinary about their trips.

"Apparently, my mom bought the lake house we used to rent during our summer visits here. It was something she did right before she died, though she never said anything to me about it. Maybe she never got the chance."

He stared at her. "Are you telling me you inherited a lake house?" It was something she'd never bothered mentioning to him.

"I did." Reese grimaced.

Wow! "You don't sound too thrilled about it. Why's that?"

She shrugged. "I don't know. Maybe because I lost her so suddenly. The lake house was our special mother-daughter getaway. The one place in the world that wasn't peppered by our many arguments."

He reached for her hand, finally understanding. "You doing okay over there?"

"Just a little sad," she admitted. "It's the first time I've ever come here without her."

"Well, you've got me this time."

"That I do." Her smile was faint.

"We can stay some place else besides the lake house, if you'd like."

"As tempting as that sounds, it would be kind of silly, considering it's the size of a small hotel," she sighed.

You're kidding! "Really?"

"Yeah. Since I wasn't ready to come back here and face my ghosts just yet, I decided to turn it into an Air B&B three years ago, which my uncle has been managing."

He gave a long, low whistle beneath his breath. "So it'll be overflowing with guests when we arrive, eh?"

"No, not anymore. Uncle Caleb's health is declining, and he got tired of dealing with the upkeep, so it's been vacant for the last six months. Guess I'm going to have to finally decide what to do with the place."

One detail was still puzzling him more than the others. "Is there any particular reason why I'm just now hearing about this?" *Your best friend...the guy you normally tell everything.*

"Yes and no." She stared out the window. "He's

not really my uncle, though my mom always insisted I call him that." Her lips thinned in disapproval. "They were friends. Pretty close ones, apparently, after Dad died."

Ah. "So did your mom and her special friend ever, ah...?"

"Date?" Reese's blonde brows rose. "I don't know, but I intend to find out."

"Hey, now." Garek reached over to touch her shoulder. "I'm all for getting in touch with your roots, darling, but sometimes it's best not to dig too deep." That was something his single mom had drummed into his brain every time he asked too many questions about his jailbird of a father. Sometimes it was best to leave the past in the past.

"You're probably right," Reese sighed, blindly squeezing his hand. "How about we just focus on getting ready for our first episode?"

"I can do that." Garek laced his fingers through hers and rested their joined hands on his knee. "What was the address again?" He'd been watching the building numbers for the past few minutes. They had to be getting close.

"It's 3001 Heart Lake Circle. Just so you know, the building we're looking for isn't really a lake house. It actually used to be one of those old mills."

Garek gave a huff of disbelief as a building with that number on it drew into sight. Reese was right. It looked nothing like a residential home. The massive story-and-a-half wooden structure was as big as a warehouse. It was in good condition, though, sporting a fresh coat of redwood stain.

The single story wing of it jutted over the frozen lake on a dozen or more stone piers. The two-story portion boasted a set of double doors bearing pine wreaths. On the east side of the building was a trio of tarnished silver silos. It was hard to tell from this angle if they were still operable or if they'd simply been left in place for their historic beauty.

"I've never been here in December, but Uncle Caleb was right." Reese sounded relieved as she peered in fascination through the windshield. "With the snow on the roof and the frozen lake in the background, it practically screams it's the holidays. It's the perfect backdrop for filming our pre-show teasers."

Our pre-show. Garek liked how she'd included him in that statement. And he couldn't agree more with her assessment of the mill house. Heart Lake was undeniably the perfect place to film a Christmas show. Shoot! The property wouldn't even require much staging. Every snow-spattered spruce and pine towering over the mill looked like a Christmas tree. He and his film crew could probably get away with tossing up a few strands of lights and be done with it.

"Omigosh, Garek!" Reese's fingers tightened on his. "Are those Christmas lights on the eaves?"

"Think so." He squinted at the roofline as he

drove up the paved driveway. Someone had either shoveled or blown the snow away for them.

She gave a delighted chuckle. "After all of Uncle Caleb's complaining, I was expecting the place to be overgrown with vines and climbing with cobwebs. Looks like I was wrong. All we're going to have to do is assemble the equipment and start filming."

"After we replace the one contestant who quit," Garek reminded. For two weeks straight, they'd been advertising that they would be holding local tryouts two days from now.

Four empty parking spots yawned in the barn-like building without doors at the end of the drive-way. None of them were deep enough for Garek to pull the SUV inside with the trailer hitched. However, they were big enough to park each rig separately.

The front door of the mill flew open, and a swarthy-skinned man on a cane hobbled outside to the porch. He was wearing a fringed suede tunic, and his long dark hair swung like a curtain around his shoulders. There was no mistaking his Native American roots.

"That's him," Reese said excitedly.

The moment Garek pulled on the emergency brake, she slid her hand free of his and leaped from the vehicle. "Uncle Caleb!" she called, flying in his direction. For someone who wasn't actually related to her, Reese seemed pretty glad to see him.

It made Garek wonder all over again why she'd never mentioned the man to him. He followed at a slower pace, giving them time to enjoy the reunion of old friends. As his boots crunched over the well-salted driveway, the front door flew open again. This time, a younger man stepped out. He was as swarthy as the older man. However, he wasn't wearing fringed leather. He was in jeans and a Stetson like Garek. Well, not exactly like Garek, since his white button-up shirt boasted a shiny police badge.

The plot thickens. Garek stiffened as the younger guy leaned over to give Reese a not-too-brief bear hug. *Alright. That's long enough, buddy.* Garek's patience was wearing thin with the whole family-that-wasn't-really-a-family reunion. It was past time to announce his own presence, a best friend who was really a best friend.

"Hello!" He raised a hand in greeting as he strode across the short sidewalk to the porch.

Reese glanced laughingly his way. "There you are. I wondered what was taking you so long."

Every cell in Garek bristled at the way the younger guy still had his arm slung casually around her waist.

Meanwhile, her Uncle Caleb was eyeing him in suspicion. "And you are?"

"Garek Borden, my business partner," Reese said quickly.

Business partner, eh? It was the first time she'd

ever introduced him publicly as such. Garek scanned her gaze as he mounted the porch steps. She had him on a generous salary and included him in nearly every facet of the affairs surrounding Max West Adventures. However, they both knew it wasn't an official partnership, though it was something he was very open to discussing later if she was serious.

She smiled sunnily back at him. "He's also my best friend, chief sound boarder, and head camera guy, among other things."

Boy, she was really pouring it on. Garek waggled his brows at their listeners, more curious than ever about what she was up to. "Almost feels like I should take a bow."

"Sounds like an impressive resume." The older gentleman stiffly held out a hand to Garek. "I'm Caleb Whitaker. An old friend of Sheree's." His handshake was stronger than Garek was expecting. "And this is my nephew, Shep. He works for the Heart Lake Police Department," he added with no small amount of pride.

"Deputy Shep Whitaker, an old friend of Reese's," Shep supplied easily. He leaned forward to shake Garek's hand without dropping his arm from Reese's waist. "We go way back. She and her mom vacationed here every summer during high school."

Garek nearly laughed when Shep gave him one of those firm macho handshakes, just shy of breaking bones. *Got something to prove, eh?* "Reese and I have lived next door to each other since the day we were born, so we go *all* the way back."

Shep quickly dropped Garek's hand, looking a little less confident than before.

"Well, it's great to see you again. Both of you." Reese leaned in to give Shep a quick squeeze hug before stepping away from him to face Garek. She held a wide chrome key ring in front of him and shook it to make the set of keys on it jingle.

"Uncle Caleb just handed me the keys to the place, though I sincerely hope this doesn't mean he intends to abandon us altogether during our visit."

When she didn't lower her hand, Garek presumed she wanted him to hang onto the keys for her. Nodding, he accepted them and tucked them inside the pocket of his jeans.

The exchange elicited dark looks from both of the Whitaker men.

Uncle Caleb angled his head at the double front doors. "It's as cold as the North Pole out here. How about we take this visit inside?"

Garek carefully edged his taller frame in between Shep and Reese, hovering shamelessly near her as they passed over the threshold and stepped inside.

"Oh, wow!" Reese breathed, spinning in a full circle in the entry foyer. "It's even more beautiful than I remember."

Garek watched her indulgently. "I bet it looks a lot different with snow and Christmas lights."

She nodded merrily. "It does."

Uncle Caleb beckoned them to follow him into what turned out to be a great room. Twin deer antler chandeliers were suspended from the ceilings, and an array of leather furniture and animal skin rugs were scattered across the rustic hardwood floor. "Your mother thought it was beautiful in every season. She always swore it was the place she would retire to when her sailing days were over."

Reese's gasp echoed all the way to the cathedral ceiling and back, and her face grew so pale that Garek leaped to her side. "A glass of water, please," he ordered tersely.

"I'm okay, Garek," she murmured shakily as he stepped backward with her and gently deposited her on the wide cushion of one of the leather sofas. "I'm okay," she repeated in a whisper as he took a knee in front of her. "It's just a bit of a shock discovering that she planned to retire here."

If it's even true. He stubbornly remained where he was, rubbing his thumb in gentle circles over the top of her hand until Shep returned.

The deputy was holding a tall glass bottle of sparkling water. "It's from the gift shop down the street," he announced brightly. "Your favorite brand."

"Thanks." Garek swiped it from his outstretched

hand without meeting his gaze and unscrewed the cap. Holding the bottle to Reese's trembling lips, he ordered, "Drink."

She closed her eyes as she took a few sips. Her lashes fluttered against her cheeks for a moment before raising her gaze again to her uncle. "My mom never mentioned her plans to retire here. I'll admit it was a surprise to hear you say that."

"She was a woman of many secrets." Uncle Caleb, who'd remained standing in the entryway up to this point, thumped his cane across the room and dropped into the leather armchair across from her.

Wondering if one of Sheree Summerville's secrets was a romantic entanglement with the gnarled Uncle Caleb, Garek half-rose to perch on the arm of the sofa next to Reese. Together, they faced the man who might've become her step-father if her mother had lived longer.

"Sheree loved it here," he mused in a melancholy voice. "Said it was the best mother-daughter time the two of you had ever enjoyed."

Garek did a quick mental calculation. If Reese and her mother had visited here during her high school years, that would've been right after her father had passed of lung cancer.

"Our vacations here were pretty awesome, yes." The water bottle shook in Reese's hand. "We picnicked out on the lake and took long walks in the starlight. She never said anything to me about buying the place, though, or retiring here. Was there, er, another reason she might've..." Her voice dwindled uncertainly.

"I don't think she planned anything very far in advance." The older gentleman smiled sadly. "She lived in the moment, followed her heart, and left this world without too many regrets. I'm sure of it."

"You sound like you knew my mom pretty well," Reese sighed.

His expression grew shuttered, making Garek suspect that there had, in fact, been more to his relationship with Reese's mother than friendship.

As if tired of being left out of the conversation, Shep plunged back in. "These lake lots are in pretty big demand. They don't go for sale often. And when they do, they don't last long on the market."

"Are you the one who told her about it going for sale?" Reese asked her uncle curiously.

"Actually, no. If I understood correctly, your father brought her here for the first time many years ago. He's the one who secured a realtor to notify them if the place ever went up for sale." The papery skin around his mouth twisted in something akin to disapproval.

Garek studied him shrewdly, suddenly wondering if Uncle Caleb's feelings that went beyond friendship had been one-sided. If that was the case, Sheree Summerville may have come to Heart Lake with her daughter to chase after her husband's ghost. Maybe it had been the one place the three of them could be together again, at least in her memories.

Heath Summerville had been one of the top fire chiefs in Dallas. Garek remembered him well. He was the main reason Garek had decided to become a volunteer firefighter — to both honor his memory and to impress the man's daughter. Boy, had that backfired!

Reese darted a glance up at Garek from her perch on the sofa. "Well, it's good to be back. I can't wait to show the town off to the rest of our crew when they arrive."

"It's good to have you back." Uncle Caleb's smile disappeared as his dark gaze flickered to Garek. "I reckon you can bunk your staff over the garage. In the old days, it was one big dormitory room, but it's since been upgraded to an apartment with all the modern conveniences."

Garek was amused by the man's thinly veiled hint that her business partner fit into the category of hired help.

Reese nodded eagerly. "The rest of our crew will be driving into town tomorrow. They're brothers living out of an RV, so they'll probably rig some hookups in the driveway. But Garek," she arched her brows knowingly at him, "won't mind commandeering the apartment space you mentioned."

"You know it," he assured with a grin, liking the

idea of having so much space to himself. It was a lot better than being stuck for months on end in a tiny hotel room. "Since my partner always piles on the projects, I prefer to work as close to home base as possible."

"I see." Mr. Whitaker's voice was as dry as a stick of firewood as he stood. "Well, I'm going to mosey on home, but Shep can stick around as long as you need to answer any questions you have about the place. He's been doing most of the upkeep for me in recent months." He waved in irritation at his lame knee.

Despite the man's crankiness, Garek leaped to his feet and hurried into the foyer to hold open the front door for him.

Mr. Whitaker paused atop the threshold, allowing the icy December breeze to swirl inside. "So you're her business partner, eh?" He seemed to be weighing the notion.

"That's one way of putting it." Garek shrugged. "She means the world to me, sir." To discourage any matchmaking plans the older fellow might have for Reese and his nephew, Garek didn't mind dropping a hint that he intended to become more.

Mr. Whitaker harrumphed. "Sheree mentioned you a few times, but it was always in the past tense."

"Interesting." Their gazes clashed. "Neither she nor Reese ever mentioned you at all."

CHAPTER 3: TESTING THE WATERS
REESE

Thumbs dangling from the belt loops of his jeans, Shep Whitaker studied Reese as Garek left the room with his uncle. He angled his head at the wide entryway leading to the hallway. "So you finally found a guy you couldn't live without, eh?" No small amount of curiosity was etched into his bronze Native American features.

Marveling in the many changes he'd undergone since they'd last seen each other, she chuckled at his reference to the foolish claim she'd made to him back in high school — that she'd never met a guy she couldn't live without. "I can't believe you even remember that conversation." She abruptly set her water bottle on the nearest end table and sprang up from the sofa. "We were barely more than kids."

"Maybe you're just an unforgettable kind of gal." He lounged back against the stacked stone fireplace as she started to pace the spacious room. His former shoulder-length brown hair was gone. In its place was a sports cut. It was closely shaved on the sides and long enough on top to wave a bit. He was taller than she remembered, too.

Uncomfortable with the more intimate turn of their conversation, Reese moved to a trio of carved antique bookcases to run a hand over the spines of a few dozen Zane Grey novels. Her fingertips collected no dust, indicating that the mill house had been cleaned recently.

"I still can't believe this place is mine," she murmured, feeling dazed all over again. Being back inside it after all those years of being away made it seem a lot more real.

"It's been yours for the past three years," Shep pointed out. "Sure took you long enough to come pay us a visit."

Reese shook her head without looking up from the books. "It's been tough the last few years." She'd purposefully dragged her feet about returning to Heart Lake. She'd known it wouldn't be the same without her mother. "Guess I wasn't ready to before now."

"Well, I'm glad you finally decided to come."

Shep's voice was closer than she anticipated, making Reese jolt. She glanced up to find him standing right beside her. He was holding out a sealed white envelope.

"Sorry." His chuckle was low and rumbly with affection. "Didn't mean to scare you."

"What's this?" She reached for the envelope, wishing he'd give her a little more space. They weren't in high school anymore, and the summer fun they'd enjoyed together felt like a lifetime ago.

"Combinations to the gate locks, that sort of thing. I asked Uncle Caleb if I could be the one to give it to you, so we could talk. I hope you don't mind."

Talk? Her eyes widened at how serious he sounded. "Not at all. Why would I?" Surely he wasn't still hung up on their last conversation. It was a crazy long time ago.

He grimaced. "Well, you have to admit it was a little awkward the way we parted last time."

Yep. He was going there. "That was a long time ago, Shep." She made a face at him, not sure why he felt the need to bring it up again. "You asked me out, and I was totally flattered. For reals. But I didn't want to do the long distance thing."

"And now you're back," he pointed out quietly.

"Only for a few months," she said quickly. "My job pretty much requires me to stay on the road." Uncle Caleb's refusal to continue in his role as care-taker for her mill house B&B was adding a whole new and interesting wrinkle to her already compli-cated life. She'd have to decide if she was going to keep the place or sell it. It was a good thing that

Garek had agreed to film the winter season of their show here. At least she would have him by her side while she debated what to do with the property.

"I thought you loved it here." He sounded taken aback.

She stared at him, wondering what in the world he'd been trying to read into her return to Heart Lake. *What am I missing?* "I do love it here. Heart Lake is a gorgeous town. However, until Uncle Caleb suggested we come film the next season of our show here, it was just a vacation spot."

"I think he was hoping — or rather, *we* were hoping that your return meant more."

She shook her head in puzzlement. "I really am here to film a show, Shep, and hopefully to find a new property manager during that time. If I can't, then I'm going to have another really tough decision ahead."

"By tough decision, you mean putting the property up for sale, don't you?" He sounded both disappointed and disapproving.

"I honestly don't know."

"See?" A slow grin lit his features. "This place means something to you, maybe more than you realize."

"Of course it does." *But I just rolled into town a few minutes ago, remember?* She wasn't making any decisions today, tomorrow, or the next day. It was going to take a lot of soul-searching to decide what to do with one of her last ties to her mother.

Shep stuffed his hands in his pockets, looking more like his old carefree self. "Well, if you decide to unload it, you won't have any trouble. There's a waiting list a mile long for people wanting to snap up these lake lots."

"Does that include you?" She shot him a curious glance.

"Nope." He snorted. "Sheesh, woman! Cops aren't made of gold." He rocked back on the heels of his boots as he gazed around them. "Plus, I happen to be more of a cabin-in-the-woods kinda guy, in case you've forgotten."

"Right." His uncle had been crippled during a bull riding accident, ending his rodeo days. Shep had been taking care of him ever since, first on his high school grocery bagger wages and eventually on his police salary. The last time she'd visited Heart Lake, they were living in a very humble cottage on the edge of town. Shep was truly an amazing person, just not someone she'd ever seen herself dating.

Jobs like hers didn't leave a lot of time for a social life. Reese twisted the white envelope in her hands, unsure of what to say next.

Fortunately, Garek chose that moment to stroll back into the great room. His brown gaze moved between the two of them and turned steely. "Hey,

Shep," he drawled. "Any chance you'd like to serve as one of our contestants on Max West Adventures?"

Shep's swarthy features turned incredulous. "Not a chance." He reached up to tap his silver star. "This badge means I'm one of the guys that folks like you call to run rescue ops through the mountains."

Folks like you. His meaning was painfully clear. Reese bit her lower lip. It wasn't the first time she and Garek had been accused of being bored city slickers looking for their next thrill. However, they didn't usually argue the matter. They just smiled all the way to the bank. The survivalist show business had turned out to be a wildly profitable venture.

Garek shrugged. "If you change your mind, let us know. Our sponsors are very generous, so the winning pot this season is going to be our biggest one yet."

Despite his effort to remain nonchalant, interest prickled in Shep's dark gaze. "Like I said, my job takes top priority. If I did have time to burn, however, what all would this gig entail?"

It was nice seeing something besides disdain in his expression for Max West Adventures. Reese brightened as she described their upcoming show schedule. "There will be a dozen contestants in the first round, which will be a forty-eight-hour Winter Woodsman Challenge."

"Let me guess," Shep interjected in a teasing voice. "We'll have to live off the land for a full two days with nothing more than three matches and a pocket knife."

She chuckled. "Close, but our contestants will have a few more supplies than that."

"Aha. Four matches instead of three." He smirked.

Still grinning, she waggled a finger. "And once the contestants are good and cold—"

"And hungry," he added.

"Yes. Cold *and* hungry," she agreed, "then comes the bungee jump over the canyon."

"You're kidding!" His dark brows flew upward. "What's the point of that? To ensure everyone is frozen solid?"

She spread her hands. "Our contestants tend to fall in one of two categories — those with spines of steel and those with spines of titanium. Plus, our viewers expect to be entertained. So a bungee jump over such spectacular terrain is a win-win. Everyone goes home happy, and one person goes home a lot richer." Recalling Shep's earlier comment about how cops weren't made of money, she narrowed her gaze on him. If he could finagle the time off, he'd seriously be the perfect candidate for her show.

He rolled his eyes at her. "Quit looking at me like that."

"You'd give the other contestants a real run for their money."

"Yes, I would." He moved toward the entry

foyer. "It would be like stealing candy from a baby, though. This country boy knows these mountains like the back of his hand."

"Is that a yes?" she called gayly after him.

"It's an I'll-think-about-it." He paused to tap his fist against the door frame. "You're only looking for one more contestant, right?"

"That is correct. The other candidates were slated months ago." She glanced at Garek for confirmation, just to be sure they hadn't had any other contestants back out.

He nodded. "The only reason we have an opening on the show for this season is due to a last-minute cancellation. The guy had a family emergency."

"Sorry to hear it." Shep's tone was noncommittal, though Reese could tell he was mulling over their offer.

"Sorry for what he's going through," she agreed, "but not sorry for the opportunity to hold a final set of tryouts. This could be fun." She would seriously love to fill their last open slot with a local contestant. It would give the town a more vested interest in the show if they had some real skin in the game.

Shep didn't answer for so long that her heart sank. Maybe she'd misread his interest. "When?" he finally asked without turning around.

Or maybe not. Her heart fluttered with excitement. "Day after tomorrow. Eight o'clock sharp at the arena."

He nodded and waved two-fingers in the air instead of saying goodbye. Moments later, she heard the front door open and shut as he let himself out.

"I hope he shows up," she murmured to Garek. *Holy moly!* A hunky local cop on her show would really jazz things up. Not to mention, Shep was a really great guy. Nothing would make her happier than to watch a hardworking public servant like him win the big pot.

"Me, too." Garek pointed at the white envelope in her hand. "What's that?"

"Oh, ah..." She glanced down. "According to Shep, it's a list of gate combination codes and stuff. We can check them out and make sure they work during our grand tour of the mill house." Nostalgia rolled through her at the thought of seeing the whole place again — every four-poster bed and patchwork quilt, every antique toy and clock.

"You ready to get started on that now?"

"I think I need a few more minutes," she confessed ruefully. Shep had brought up a lot of sensitive points in their conversation. "I guess I'm still absorbing being back."

"Understood." Instead of leaving her alone like she expected and heading back outside to the trailer, Garek strode across the room. Holding out his arms, he muttered, "Come here, you."

She stepped gratefully into them.

As he folded her within the safe cocoon of his embrace, the uncertainties surrounding them lightened a few degrees.

He spoke against her hairline. "I'll admit I was a little surprised when you chose this town for our next season, but it's everything you said it was. It's the perfect terrain to film Max West Adventures."

"It is." She nodded against his shoulder. "By the end of the season, though, I'll have to figure out what to do about being saddled with a house the size of a small hotel. I can't believe Uncle Caleb is resigning as my property manager. He's really leaving me in the lurch."

Laughter rumbled through Garek's chest. "Most people would kill to have this kind of problem."

She smiled. "Probably."

His arms tightened around her. "I don't think there's any need to overthink it. Let's just enjoy using the place as our headquarters for now. You'll have plenty of time in the days ahead to weigh the pros and cons of selling versus keeping it."

His words surprised her. "You actually think I should consider keeping it?" He knew her job made her something of a rolling stone.

"I do." His voice turned serious. "It sounds like this place really meant something to you and your mother. You have a lot of happy memories here."

It was funny how Shep had pretty much said the

same thing. "I do," she sighed. "It was the one place on earth we seemed to be able to escape the sadness of losing Dad."

"There's nothing quite like a summer fling to offer a little distraction from your troubles, eh?" Garek teased.

The stiffening of his shoulders was at odds with the lightness of his words, however. "I don't know what you're talking about."

"What about you and Shep? He seems like a little more than a friend."

"Seriously? That's news to me," she lied, burrowing a little deeper into Garek's embrace. He cuddled her closer still, making a delicious shiver run through her. It was followed by a tiny spurt of alarm. She'd probably launched herself into his arms a thousand other times, but this was the first time she could recall noticing the hard planes of his chest and the corded muscles in his arms — certainly not something a BFF was supposed to be thinking about.

He sighed. "I'm not sure what the big deal is. If you like the guy, you like the guy. Just admit it already."

"Of course I like Shep," she exploded, raising her head from Garek's shoulder. "He's a wonderful person and probably a really great cop, based on what I remember about him. He's just not..." She was having trouble putting her feelings about him into words.

"You know you can tell me anything," Garek reminded patiently.

With a breathy expulsion, she disengaged herself from his arms. "Good, because there's something I've been wanting to tell you for a while."

"You're going to start dating Shep Whitaker?"

"What? No!"

"Ah. I get it now. You're secretly already dating him."

She scowled. "Can you be serious for two seconds straight?"

"I am being serious. What's wrong with dating Shep? I'm pretty sure he'd be open to the idea."

"Maybe. He did ask me out once."

"Aha! I knew it." Garek waggled a finger at her.

"I turned him down."

"When was this?"

"Back in high school." Her lips tightened. "But I didn't want a long distance relationship, so nothing ever happened." It was suddenly and inexplicably very important to her for him to believe what she was saying.

He looked amused. "Well, now you're back in the same town."

"True, but — omigosh, Garek! If you'll just listen."

"Listening." He reached for her hands. "For real this time."

"Okay. Here goes." She drew a deep breath.

"Seeing Shep again made me realize something." She squeezed Garek's hands, and he squeezed back. "After Dad died, I had a really hard time getting back to being a normal teenager, and I'm not sure that I ever did. I didn't feel like hanging out with friends anymore. Didn't feel like I had anything to offer in a relationship, which is why I never dated much. A loss like that is truly paralyzing."

"I know. I was there," he reminded softly.

"Just about the time I was coming to grips with the loss of my dad, that's when I lost my mom." She toyed with his fingers. "And the numbness started all over again."

"How does Shep fit into all of this?" he asked quietly.

She drew her brows together. "He doesn't. Why do you ask?"

"You said seeing him again was what made you realize something important."

"I just meant he made me realize how broken I am."

Garek used their joined hands to tug her closer. "Okay, darling. On that, we're going to have to disagree."

"Oh, come on, Garek! You know what I mean. I stopped dating and let my social life die a slow, horrible death. You're the only one I let in during the last three years while I was grieving, and now I don't know how to put myself back out there." She struggled to come up with the right words. "To live again."

His eyes were two dark pools of understanding. However, the usual level of empathy was missing from his voice. "It's like diving into the deep end of a pool. You just have to jump and start treading water, babe."

"That's not my style, and you know it." Her tone was cautious. "I've always preferred to trail my fingers in the water first."

"Well, what do you have in mind?" He looked intensely curious.

"I was kind of hoping you would be willing to help me make that big leap."

"How?"

"You're still my best friend, right?"

"Always."

"Who has apparently had thoughts about kissing me."

"Once or twice." He chuckled. "Does that bother you?"

"Maybe we should just do it." She held his gaze uncertainly.

"You mean kiss?" He looked astounded.

"Yes, and get it over with."

"Ouch!" His jaw dropped.

She flushed. "I didn't mean it like that. I just meant we wouldn't have to keep wondering. You know...about what it would be like."

His expression turned cunning. "So you *have* thought about kissing me."

"Well, yeah. But only after you brought it up," she returned in an accusing voice.

"Let me get this straight." He looked like he was trying not to laugh. "You think it's my fault that you want to kiss me?"

"Totally." She tilted up her chin and shook back her ponytail.

"Are you sure you're sure this is what you want?" His voice deepened with some unnamed emotion.

"Only if you'll promise me that a single kiss won't send you running for the hills." She gave him a nervous smile. "I can't afford to lose my lead camera guy right before our season opening."

"Double ouch! I'm back to being your lowly cameraman, huh?" he teased.

"Are you always going to be this difficult?"

"Yes." He dipped his head over hers. "Giving you a hard time about stuff is one of the coolest perks of being your best friend."

She was relieved he wasn't actually all weirded out about her crazy request. "Are you going to kiss me or what?"

"I'm considering it." He lowered his head another inch over hers.

"You really do have to promise we'll still be friends."

"I promise. Can't guarantee it won't change things between us, though."

She frowned. "What do you mean?"

"Well, for one thing, you might find that you like kissing me, in which case one kiss will never be enough."

"And that's a bad thing, you cocky cowboy?"

"I didn't say that."

"Well, there's only one way to find out." She swayed closer to him. "I'm seriously never going to get back in the dating game if you don't help me."

"Why do I suddenly feel like I'm being used?" he teased.

"Just shut up and do it already!" Reese stood on her tiptoes to brush her lips against his.

All the joking between them ceased as Garek's hard mouth moved over hers, ever so tenderly kissing her back. All too soon, it was over. He lifted his head. "Well? What do you think?"

Heart pounding, she stared at him. "That's it?" Disappointment crashed into her. It was too short. She'd been expecting a little more from a guy who'd been friends with her so long.

His black brows rose. "Good grief, Reese! I kissed you back. That's what you wanted, isn't it?" He studied her with genuine concern.

"I guess." She knew she was being unreasonable, but she couldn't help it. "I just thought we were going to—"

"Do this?" Without warning, Garek swooped back in for another kiss. This time, his mouth moved over hers much more slowly. It was like he was drinking her in. With one arm, he hooked her closer. Then he tenderly cupped her face and deepened their kiss.

Yes! Like this. Reese suddenly felt like laughing and crying at the same time. This was it — everything she'd missed out on during the past several years, everything she'd daydreamed about during those wistful little stolen moments. Nothing in her wildest imagining, however, compared with the breathless wonder, the infinite longing, the overpowering sweetness of a real kiss.

Garek raised his head a fraction. "Better?" he inquired huskily. He dragged his thumb with devastating gentleness along the underside of her chin.

"So much better," she whispered, wishing they could revel in the enchantment of their first kiss forever. "And you're still my best friend?" she asked anxiously.

"Yep." He tucked her head beneath his chin and rocked her gently from side to side. "So how did it rate?"

"Wh-what?" She stirred in his arms.

"My kiss."

"Oh! Am I supposed to give it five stars or something?" A shaky chuckle escaped her.

"I was hoping for more like ten stars or twenty,

but yeah. I'm a guy. I wouldn't mind knowing how my kiss measured up to your other ones."

"Seriously? How many guys do you think I've kissed?" She raised her head from his shoulder, blushing furiously.

"Too many," he growled.

"Well, I haven't." Gosh, this was embarrassing, but she'd never been anything less than honest with him.

"What about Shep?"

"What about him?"

"Did he kiss you?"

"No. You're the only, um..." She broke off, flustered.

He looked amazed. "Are you trying to tell me I'm the only guy you've ever kissed?"

"Well, there was little Timmy in kindergarten, and Matt Keefer in the third grade, but yeah. You're the only one since then."

"No kidding!" Garek couldn't have looked more floored. "Wow! I'm honored. Really."

She snickered. "I think you're more surprised than honored."

"You've been on dates, Reese. How was I supposed to know you've never kissed any of the poor fellas at the end of the night?"

She shrugged. "You of all people should know how cautious I am. Dating is no exception to that rule."

"Right." He grinned. "Hey, uh, I'm still waiting for you to rate my kiss."

"Now you're just fishing."

"Without shame, darling."

"I can't," she teased back. "I have nothing to compare it to."

He rested his hands lightly on her waist. "I could kiss you again," he offered, looking innocent. "Then you could tell me which one of the two was better."

"I, ah..." She felt suddenly tongue-tied. "Okay."

"Really?"

"Yes." She swayed closer.

This time, his kiss was blatantly more possessive and very, very thorough. By the time he raised his head, both of them were having trouble breathing normally. "So?" he asked in a voice rough with emotion.

"I'm still too new at this," she whispered. "Again, please."

CHAPTER 4: UNCHARTERED TERRITORY

GAREK

Garek lost track of the number of times he kissed Reese. All he knew was that he didn't want to stop. Ever. It took every ounce of his willpower to lift his head enough to smile against her lips. "That trailer's not going to unload itself." Somehow he'd ended up with his back against the bookcase with a few dozen book spines digging into his shoulder blades, not that he minded. She had her arms twined around his neck like she never wanted to let him go.

"Probably not." She didn't sound in any more of a hurry than he was to end their impromptu necking session. As she slowly tipped her head back against his arm, the look in her eyes made him feel bullet-proof and a thousand feet tall.

"You're really gonna have to stop looking at me like that if you want me to get any work done." He ran his thumb beneath her chin for the last time and forced himself to lower his hand to his side. Wow! He was Reese's first kiss. The wonder of that discovery was still sinking in.

"I'll try," she murmured dreamily. "Please assure me again that we're still best friends."

"We are."

"Good. Because I don't want to lose you, Garek."

"I'm not going anywhere."

"But you will," she sighed. "Eventually."

He raised his eyebrows at her.

"When you fall in love. It could happen, you know."

He stared at her, momentarily at a loss for words. It was the last thing he'd expected her to say after what they'd just shared. The ensuing crash of disappointment nearly staggered him.

"Why are you looking at me like that?" She scowled up at him.

"Because you just..." He shook his head in disgust at her.

"Kissed you, I know," she sighed, "after which you assured me we were still best friends. So please stop looking at me like I've ruined everything between us."

No, baby. Ruining things doesn't even come close to describing what you did. She'd set his entire world on fire, then she'd acted like it was no big deal. He felt like shaking her. "I warned you that kissing me could change things between us."

She looked stricken. "Okay. Go ahead and lay it on me. How bad have I messed things up?"

"I didn't say you messed anything up, darling. I said you changed things."

"Oka-a-ay." She still looked so uncertain that he almost laughed.

"I've wanted to kiss you for a long time, Reese, and I already want to kiss you again."

"Oh." She blushed — hard. "Um, wow!" She unwound her arms from his neck and took a stumbling step back.

"Yeah. Wow! I couldn't have said it better. Unlike you, I've kissed a few frogs, so I understand exactly how incredible our kisses were." He pushed away from the bookcase to bring them closer again.

"Really?" Her eyes shone with so much pleasure at the simple compliment that he nearly yanked her back in his arms to kiss her senseless right then and there.

"Really, really." He could still feel the imprint of her warm, soft lips against his. "What we have between us is special. Very special." He grinned down at her. "So special that I'm willing to wager you could kiss a dozen other guys in the next week without experiencing anything close to what just happened between us."

Her blue eyes widened in shock. "You want me to kiss a dozen other guys?"

"Actually, I'd prefer that you don't." He chuckled. "Maybe you could just take my word for it."

"So where does this leave things between us?" She bit her lower lip worriedly.

"You've always been my best friend, Reese Summerville. After today, though, you're a little more than that."

Relief flooded her heart-shaped features. "I can live with more, Garek, just not less," she confessed shyly.

"Good, because there's no putting what just happened between us back in the bottle." Not in a million years.

Her smile turned wicked. "Just so long as you understand I refuse to give up any of my rights."

His heart sank. *Here it comes.* He fully expected her to spell out the ground rules for remaining a single woman.

"I reserve the right to speak my mind to you about all things concerning Max West Adventures. I also reserve the right to argue back any time you make me mad."

Something warm and wonderful twisted in his heart. "I reckon that's what make-up kisses are for." He couldn't wait to show her.

"Is that all you're ever going to think about from now on?" she demanded. "Kissing me again?"

"Pretty much." He raised and lowered his shoulders, monumentally unconcerned with how much distress his confession might be causing her. "If it's any comfort, it's all I've thought about for a very long time, so it's really nothing new."

She blushed again. "Is that why you gave up that other really great job offer?"

"Yes."

"And agreed to come with me to Heart Lake?"

"For sure." He reached out to tuck a strand of hair behind her ear. "I believe in you, and I believe in Max West Adventures. There's no place I'd rather be than by your side forever and always."

An arrested expression stole across her features. "Does this mean you'll actually consider that partnership I've been dropping hints about?"

He curled his upper lip at her. "Only if you're capable of giving up the joys of being my boss. Heaven knows you've enjoyed lording your position over me the last few years," he joked.

"I have not!" she gasped. "I've never thought of you as anything besides an equal when it comes to professional stuff."

"What about personal stuff?" he pressed.

"Well, obviously I'm still trying to figure out the personal stuff." She sounded breathless again. "Sheesh, Garek! You were my first kiss. I honestly don't know what this makes us or what's even supposed to come next."

"I have a few ideas."

"Just be patient with me, alright?" she pleaded. "I was pretty honest about needing to test the water first."

He jutted his chin at her. "All I'm trying to figure out is if you expect me to watch from the sidelines while a bunch of other guys drool and paw all over you, because that's not gonna happen. No way." He was seeing red just thinking about it.

"I can't help what other guys think or do," she declared breathlessly.

"What if Officer Shep Whitaker decides to make another play for you?" he demanded.

A smile tugged at her lips. "You seem really hung up on Shep."

"Only because he seems really hung up on you."

"I hope he doesn't ask me out again, okay?" She reached up and touched his cheek. "That's not what I want."

He reached up to imprison her hand there. "I thought you didn't know what you wanted."

"Well, I know what I don't want, and I don't want to date Shep. Is that what you needed to hear?"

He clenched his jaw, trying to be satisfied with her answer. "Guess I better brace myself for the next time I have to watch him flirting with you."

"I won't be flirting back," she assured, scanning his features anxiously.

"I'd appreciate that." He lowered her hand from

his face, but didn't yet let it go. "Different topic. While your Uncle Caleb was bragging about his nephew, he happened to let slip that the Heart Lake Police Department's new Search and Rescue Team is pretty short-handed right now. All they have is a handful of officers and one high school apprentice. I thought I might volunteer my services while we're in town, assuming you don't have a problem with that."

She chuckled. "They're about to be even more short-handed if Shep decides to try out for our show."

"So you think it's a fair trade?" He waggled his eyebrows at her.

"Only if you don't complain too loudly about me tagging along." She lifted her chin in challenge.

"I should've known you'd find a way to finagle something out of this for yourself," he mused, shaking his head.

"Yep." She clapped her hands excitedly. "I'll get to play with the cute little doggies and everything."

He shook his head at her. "Number one. They're not lap dogs. Number two—"

"Save it, Mr. Crabby Pants." She rolled her eyes. "I was kidding about playing with the rescue dogs. I know they have one mission, and that's to save lives, which is exactly why I want to learn more about it. Skills like this could prove to be very useful in our line of business."

"Alright, then." He couldn't argue with that.

"They said they start training at seven o'clock sharp each morning, Monday through Friday. Are you game for rolling out of bed that soon?"

"So long as you agree to vouch for me when we get there. I doubt anyone at the PD is going to take a survivalist reality TV hostess very seriously on her own merits."

"Done. Preparing to vouch. Anything else?" He was looking forward to the prospect of sharing his search and rescue skills with her. That, and spending more time with her.

"Yes. We're probably going to need a dog to train with."

"You want your own dog?" he repeated carefully.

She nodded. "My favorite breeds are Dalmatians and Huskies, though I'll agree to work with any decent pooch you can rustle up for us on this short of notice."

"So in addition to unloading our equipment trailer before nightfall, you expect me to locate you a dog?" he growled, pretending to be outraged.

"Yes, partner." She fluttered her long lashes at him.

There she was, throwing that term around again. "Guess I better get busy."

"Guess you better." She took a step back from him. "Oh, and watch your text messages. It'll probably make the most sense to set up our film editing equipment right here in the great room." She did a quick spin, waving her hands at the wall of windows facing the mountains. "The lighting is excellent, and don't even get me started on the breathtaking view. That said," she spun back in his direction, "I'm about to take the grand tour to see what's changed. If I find a better spot for us to work, I'll let you know."

He agreed that his current view was breathtaking, but he wasn't looking at the mountains. Tipping his hat at her, he made his way toward the front door. He paused in the entryway. "Hey, do you need the keys?" He reached inside his pocket and withdrew them to jingle them at her.

She waved them away. "Why don't you hang on to them for now? You'll most likely need them to unlock the apartment over the garage. Not to mention, I'm about to call the lock company to re-key all the doors and gates, anyway. Heaven only knows how many folks have had access to the set Uncle Caleb gave us."

"Good point." He made his way out the front door and took the steps two at a time.

GAREK SPENT the next couple of hours unloading the trailer and getting their equipment set up in the great room. Despite his insistence that he could handle it, Reese followed him to the trailer several times to help carry in boxes.

He enjoyed every moment they spent together, shamelessly meeting her gaze and allowing their fingers to brush every chance he could. When they were finished emptying the trailer, she followed him to the apartment over the garage.

"This is great!" Grinning in delight, she spun in a full circle. Like the rest of the renovated mill, the space was already furnished. It had two bedrooms, a small living area, and an eat-in kitchen. Every inch of it was decorated with the same country lodge decor as the rest of the house. There were patchwork quilts on the beds and faux bear skin rugs on the floor. The bedside lamp stands boasted grizzly bear figurines in various poses — climbing the tall spruces, swinging from low-lying branches, and frolicking with their cubs. White valances of eyelet lace framed the windows. It was a clean and cozy place that had a homey feel to it.

Reese moved across the room to flip on one of the lamps. "Aren't these bears adorable?"

"Very." His gaze was on her, though.

She glanced his way, and their gazes locked and held. With a breathless chuckle, she was the first to glance away. "Are you getting hungry?"

"A little." He hadn't realized it until now. He'd been too mesmerized by how much more relaxed and contented she appeared than usual. Ever since their kissing session, she'd looked downright happy. He knew better than to read too much into that, but he was doing it, anyway.

"Okay. I'll go take a peek at what's in the kitchen back at the house. Worst-case scenario, we'll order pizza for dinner. I saw a pizzeria on our way down Main Street."

He gave her a thumbs up. "While you're figuring out food, I'm going to run a quick errand."

She looked curious, but it was too soon to get her hopes up about what he had in mind. He moved past her to the door. "I'll be back as soon as I can."

"Why so secretive all of a sudden, Mr. Borden?" She leaned over the bed to smooth a corner of the quilt into place.

"If I told you, it wouldn't still be secret," he teased back.

Minutes later, he was cruising along the main highway back to the downtown area. It wasn't difficult to find the two-story red brick building that housed the police department. It was an older structure whose bricks were weathered with age. A long canopy stretched over the porch and extended into the parking lot. Since the air was thick with snow flurries, Garek claimed the last empty spot under the canopy. Though it was unmarked, he hoped he wasn't stealing anyone's regular spot.

When he opened the front door, he had to jog up a short flight of stairs to reach the main reception area. At the top of the stairs, he found himself in a spacious, well-lit room that smelled like coffee and echoed with the constant ring of phones.

"Hi there, cowboy." A middle-aged woman glanced up from her computer and offered him a curious smile. A dimple flashed at him from the edge of her cheek. "I'm Fran Beecher. How can I help you?" Dressed in simple jeans and a plaid shirt, she smoothed a hand over her chin-length salt-and-pepper hair as she waited for his response.

He nodded at her. "I was hoping to have a word with Officer Lincoln Hudson." When she dipped her head to peer at him over the top of her reading glasses, he added, "I'm a search and rescue volunteer from Dallas. Since I'll be in town for a few months, I'd like to help out, if he needs another set of hands." Or two, since Reese wanted to volunteer as well.

"You betcha." Fran picked up her phone and punched in a number. "Linc? I have someone from Dallas who'd like to come volunteer as a search and rescue worker." She listened for a few seconds. "Not yet. He looks honest, though." She winked up at Garek. "Sure. I'll send him your way in ten."

Hanging up the phone, she motioned for him to take a seat in the empty chair next to her desk. "I'll be needing to see your driver's license and at least one other form of I.D."

He dug for his wallet.

In the promised ten minutes, she had him sign a bunch of forms in order to get his background check rolling. Then she pointed across the room at the two office doors that were propped open. "Officer Hudson's office is the one on the left."

"Thanks, Fran." He moved past a smirking auburn-haired deputy with his boots crossed on his desk. It was only Garek's opinion, but the guy looked way too young to be wearing a badge.

He gave Garek a two-fingered salute and called out, "In case no one's warned you, beware of the—"

As Garek leaned in to rap his knuckles on the door and announce his presence, a series of barks had him springing back into the main room.

An enormous Golden Retriever appeared in the doorway.

"Tried to warn you," the smug deputy chortled.

Garek grinned. "I reckon you did."

"Sit, Glory!" the dog's handler ordered sharply.

Glory sat, though she continued to watch Garek with suspicion.

A tall, blonde police officer poked his head around her. "Mr. Borden, I presume?"

Garek nodded. "You must be Officer Hudson."

"Call me Lincoln and come on in." The officer pointed in warning at his dog. "You. Stay."

Glory thumped her tail against the floor and didn't budge as Garek sidled past her.

"Man, an unexpected volunteer? It's like an early Christmas gift!" Lincoln Hudson beamed at him. "Pardon me if I seem a little over-exuberant, but we don't get many volunteers popping into the station. Not in a small town like this." Though his demeanor was friendly, he remained standing and didn't offer Garek a seat, indicating he planned to keep their meeting short.

"He means we get none," the deputy outside his office called to them laughingly. "As in zero."

"That smart aleck is Wheeler Remington, the sheriff's nephew," Lincoln explained, rolling his eyes. "Just ignore him. Everyone else does."

"Except when I'm cracking their cases wide open," the young deputy called back, "in which case, they're tripping all over me to serve me coffee."

"Only in your dreams, kiddo." Lincoln spread his hands and looked expectantly at Garek. "So how soon can you start?"

"Tomorrow morning," Garek glanced over at Glory, "assuming you have a dog my partner and I can train with."

"Two new volunteers instead of one?" Lincoln held the back of one hand over his forehead, pretending he was feeling faint.

Garek nodded firmly, fully expecting a little resistance to what he had to say next. "She's the owner of Max West Adventures."

Lincoln's expression turned doubtful. "You mean the reality show star who's friends with Shep Whitaker?"

Garek tried to mask a wince. "Yep. She's CPR

certified with a number of other credentials under her belt. I've known her my entire life and worked with her professionally for the past three years, so I can vouch for the fact that she's the real deal."

Lincoln Hudson threw up his hands. "You know what? I'm not even sure why I'm pretending to put up a fuss. We're so desperate for help around here that I would probably take her on without any experience whatsoever — so long as she passes the background check, of course."

"She will," Garek assured. *Whew!* That was one hurdle crossed. He hoped Lincoln could help him with the second one. "All we need is a dog to train with."

Officer Hudson cocked his head to size him up. "I hope you mean two dogs."

"I might if you have two dogs to spare." It definitely made more sense for him and Reese to each train with their own dog.

"Actually, I do. It's a bit of an unusual situation. About a month ago, the PD in the next county over lost a guy in the line of duty."

Garek eyed him gravely. "I'm sorry to hear it."

"We all were. My wife and I have been fostering his pair of huskies, hoping to re-home them. They're two-year-old siblings with a bit of pup still in them. Make that a lot of pup. However, they're decent dogs with a real affinity for search and rescue work."

"Sold." Garek couldn't believe his good luck. "How much do you want for them?"

Lincoln snorted. "How about you take them off my hands, start shouldering their massive food bill, and we'll call it even?"

Garek held out a hand. "You've got yourself a deal, officer." He could hardly believe his good fortune. Reese was going to be ecstatic.

Lincoln stepped around him. "Sorry to rush things, but I have a meeting I have to run to. If you'll follow me downstairs, though, I'll introduce you to the dogs real quick."

In the end, Lincoln did more than introduce Garek to the dogs. He handed over their leashes, lent him a pair of cages to carry them home inside, and threw in a half a bag of dog food for good measure.

When Garek returned to the mill house for lunch, he led the two snowy white creatures inside on their leashes. They were a frisky brother and sister, who pranced more than walked. The only way he could tell them apart was by their eyes. The brother's were lake blue, while the sister's were silver.

Reese glanced up at him and the dogs as he marched them straight into the kitchen.

"Smells good in here." His mouth started to water at whatever she had simmering on the stove.

"It's chili." Her eyes widened in amazement as they settled on the dogs. "Omigosh, Garek! Huskies?

Where in the world did you find these beautiful creatures?"

"It's kind of a long story. They're originally from Alaska, though." He waved proudly at the husky on his left. "This is Fish, and his sister is Chips."

"Fish and Chips?" She burst out laughing.

The dogs ears' perked up at the sound of their names. The female gave a short yip.

"That's what Officer Lincoln Hudson at the Heart Lake PD told me. At first I thought he was having a little fun at my expense, but the dogs clearly answer to Fish and Chips."

"That's hilarious. They're so beautiful, too," she crooned, moving forward to crouch down in front of the huskies.

"Be careful," he warned. "Search and rescue dogs aren't—"

"House pets, I know." She held out her hand so the dogs could sniff it and learn her scent. "I am, however, the woman who'll be serving them bowls of chili shortly."

"Hey! What about me?" He asked in surprise.

"Don't worry. I'll serve you a bowl before Fish, but not before Chips," she announced merrily. "Ladies first."

CHAPTER 5: DOG TRAINING

REESE

The next morning, Reese threw on a fleece-lined blue sweatshirt over snow pants and padded her way to the kitchen in her sock feet. She'd never been a big fan of wearing shoes in the house, so she carried her boots in one hand. She also didn't wish to startle the dogs by clomping down the hardwood stairs in her boots at five o'clock in the morning.

It was earlier than she needed to be up, but she planned to put the extra time to good use by getting better acquainted with the rescue dogs. Garek had put them to bed for the night in their borrowed cages from the police department, which he'd conveniently stashed in the mud room around the corner from the kitchen. Since she'd be training with Fish and Chips two hours from now, she hoped to build a sliver of rapport with them before then.

The scent of coffee was her first indication that she was not the first person to wake up.

"Garek?" she called softly, as she stepped inside the kitchen.

He didn't answer. She found him hunched over his iPad at the bar, scowling his way through an email. His forearms were leaning on the granite countertop. A steaming mug of coffee rested on a cork coaster nearby — untouched from the looks of it.

"Garek?" she repeated, sensing something was wrong. She set her boots down inside the doorway and silently moved across the room in his direction.

He glanced up at her approach. His jaw was hard, his expression shuttered. "Sorry. Didn't mean to wake you. I, ah..." He glanced toward the back door. "The kitchen over the garage isn't stocked with supplies, so I came looking for coffee."

Reese was glad he'd made himself at home, though she found his demeanor unsettling. "What's wrong?"

"Who says anything is wrong?" he shot back testily.

"I do," she returned firmly, "so spill."

"Just drinking a cup of coffee." He ducked his head over his iPad again.

"Seriously, Garek? It's me," she exploded. *The girl who completely lost her mind and kissed you yesterday — too many times to keep track of.*

He flicked a hard-to-read look her way, his body

language clearly suggesting he'd rather be alone. It was way too bad for him since he happened to be sitting in her kitchen.

"Your best friend, remember?" she added in a softer voice. "If anyone can tell when something is wrong with you, it's me." *OMG! Maybe the fact that we kissed is what's wrong with you.* She stared at him, utterly perplexed. Was he having second thoughts about what had happened between them yesterday? Regrets?

"Oh, my lands, Garek!" She was dying for him to say something, anything at all. "Please tell me everything is okay with us."

His black brows flew upward. "Why wouldn't it be?"

Whew! Okay. "Because you're acting like..." she waved her hands in agitation at him, "this!"

"My dad's parole was approved." His voice was unemotional, despite the bombshell he'd just dropped between them.

"Oh, wow!" Though that was the last thing she'd been expecting to hear, his announcement left her feeling weak with relief. She was very glad his mood wasn't stemming from some spillover of remorse about kissing her yesterday. Still, the fact that his father was getting out of jail was huge. The man had been behind bars the entire time she'd known Garek and his mother.

His jaw clenched. "There's nothing wow about it."

"Okay, maybe that was a bad choice of words." Reese hopped on the stool beside him and propped an elbow on the cabinet. "How bad is this going to be for you and your mother?"

He shook his head grimly. "Not sure yet. She just informed me that she's decided to let him come home."

"That's a big deal. I know he's been gone a long time."

"It's been twenty-three years, Reese."

Her heart twisted in sympathy. Garek had been a toddler when his dad was hauled away in hand-cuffs. "I'm sorry you're having to deal with this." She reached for his hand. "I can only imagine how tough it was to find out."

Garek flinched at her touch, his face growing ravaged. "My mom is acting like it's a good thing. It's almost like she's forgotten that he was put away for armed robbery. He's no choir boy." He shook his head again. "Yet she's about to march him right through the front door of her house."

Reese squeezed his hand. "Obviously she still loves him."

"I have no idea why," he groused. "All he's done is make one bad decision after another."

"People can change," Reese offered softly,

hoping to say something that would strike the right chord in him. "Maybe he has."

He bowed his head over their joined hands. "I'm sure that's what she wants to believe."

"If it's any comfort, the parole board doesn't make those decisions lightly. Your dad's freedom is something he would've had to earn."

"I am aware. That's what I keep telling myself," he muttered. "Over and over and over again. I just wish I could believe it. When I said he's no choir boy, I meant he's no choir boy. Mom wouldn't let me so much as visit him all these years. Didn't want me anywhere near the guy, acting like it was too dangerous or something." Garek drew a heavy breath. "But that's the man she's bringing into her house and home."

Reese frowned at him. "Have you shared your concerns with her?"

"I tried to. She called in the middle of the night, and we spoke for over an hour."

"And?" Reese prodded anxiously.

"She told me not to bother trying to talk her out of it. Her mind is made up."

"Maybe you should hit the road to Dallas today and pay her a visit. Some things are best said in person." Reese's heart constricted at the thought of watching her best friend, right-hand man, and business partner drive away, especially this close to their season opening episode. However, it sounded like his mom needed him more right now.

Garek snorted. "Believe me, I offered — but she already said no to that, too."

Mirth bubbled inside of Reese. "Like mother, like son."

"What's that supposed to mean?" he growled.

"That you're just like her — stubborn."

A faint smile tugged at the edges of his mouth. "Believe me, I'd much rather be like her than him, though I'm well aware I'm a chip off both blocks." He looked as if he was tasting something rotten. "You've had your reasons for not dating much in the past. Good reasons. Well, this is my much darker and dirtier reason. I never knew for sure how much of my dad was inside me, and I didn't want to hurt any innocent women to find out."

Oh, for crying out loud! Reese hated seeing him like this. "Don't do this to yourself." She leaned in to bump shoulders with him. His hard bicep didn't budge. "Your dad's mistakes are his own. You, on the other hand, are the best person I know."

His upper lip curled. "Or maybe I've just got you fooled the way he apparently has Mom fooled."

"Just stop already." She rolled her eyes at him. "You are a truly wonderful person. End of story."

"You sure about that?" He raised his tortured gaze to hers.

"Very." An impish idea popped into her mind. "Plus, you're a good kisser."

A wave of male smugness swept his features. "I thought you said you didn't have an opinion on the topic." He swiveled on his stool to face her. "Yeah, I'm pretty sure you claimed you had nothing to compare my kisses to. Blah, blah, blah..."

"Maybe I lied." She hopped down from her stool to face him. "Girls do that sometimes, you know. They tell little white lies to protect the innocent... and sometimes their own feelings."

"You lied to me about kissing other guys?" His dark brows rose in alarm.

"No. I was referring to my ability to rate your kisses." She slid her arms around his middle and stepped closer. "I might have an opinion about them after all."

His gaze grew dark with emotion as she tipped her face up to his. "What are you trying to say, darling?"

"I want to kiss you again."

"The son of a jailbird?"

"Yes." *Please don't call yourself that.*

"A guy who might have genetic stains a mile wide and two miles deep?"

"Very sure." She instinctively knew that her approval of him was the one thing that stood a real chance at distracting him from his misery.

He shook his head in bemusement at her. "And

you've always sworn you aren't drawn to danger like your mom was."

She shrugged as she stood on her tiptoes. "Like mother, like daughter, I guess. My many flaws and inconsistencies never sent you running before. Hope they don't scare you away from me now."

"I will never run from you, Reese." His lips found hers, hungry and questing with an edge of desperation.

"If you try," she threatened between kisses, "I'll just come after you."

"You and what army?" He kissed her again, more lingeringly this time.

She smiled against his lips. "If you think for one second I'll let my head camera guy slip that easily through my fingers..."

He tipped his forehead against hers. "There's that boss lady sass again."

"You know you like it," she teased.

"Actually, I think it's pretty hot."

"You're welcome. Just wanted to remind you how useful best friends can be to have around."

He raised his head with a groan. "And now you're back to brandishing the friend card."

Only because she was too much of a coward to take things further with him just yet. She tugged at his hands to pull him from the stool. "Come on. You promised Lincoln Hudson we'd be at the police station in about..." she glanced at her watch, "thirty minutes."

"I'm still drinking my coffee," he grumbled, though he allowed her to tug him to his feet.

"That sludge?" She waved in derision at his abandoned mug. "It looks ice cold." She gave him an unsympathetic smile. "You'll just have to survive without it this morning."

"Heartless woman!"

Still smiling, she marched across the kitchen to step into her boots. "I'm going to check on the dogs. You're welcome to join me or stay in here calling me names. Whatever floats your boat, mister."

He stalked after her.

Her heart swelled with happiness as they fed and tended the dogs together, then loaded them into the back of her SUV. The sunlight glinted off the silver paint as she leaped into the passenger seat.

"Look at you." Garek climbed behind the wheel. "Forcing me to leave the house without my coffee, but still making me drive the princess around in her chariot."

Reese stuck her tongue out at him and waited until they reached the main drag of shops in the downtown area. Then she imperiously ordered him to turn into the drive-through lane of the first coffee shop she saw. She proceeded to order him the tallest mug of morning brew they offered on the menu.

"What's this?" he muttered as the woman at the window held out the enormous cup to him.

"A giant dose of caffeine for my snarling bear of a driver." Reese leaned around him to hand her credit card to the attendant, liking the perky tilt to the young woman's striped uniform hat.

"I do not snarl," Garek snarled.

"Are you listening to yourself?" Out of the corner of her eye, she watched as he breathed deeply of the hot beverage and took a tentative sip. Before he could take a second sip, however, she swiped the mug from him and settled back in the passenger seat with its delicious warmth cupped between her hands. "It's big enough to share with a friend."

He stared at her in outrage, while the attendant was trying to hand him the receipt for their purchase. She looked like she was trying not to laugh. He shook his head as he accepted the receipt. "Do you see what I have to put up with?" he demanded.

"Be nice to her," the woman advised in an unsympathetic voice. "If you're lucky, she'll share."

"Yeah, be nice to me," Reese echoed with a giggle. "You heard the lady."

"Gimme that!" He made a swipe for the cup, but she held it away from him.

One of the dogs growled from their cage in the back of the Land Rover.

"See? Even Fish and Chips think you should be nicer to me," Reese teased.

"That's it." He pulled the vehicle forward a few feet, then made a hard right turn into the nearest parking spot. Setting the emergency brake, he leaned across the console. "You want to play hard ball? Fine. Bring it on!"

He angled his head around the coffee cup she was still clutching to seal his mouth over hers.

His kiss tasted like coffee laced with sadness. When he finally raised his head, she wordlessly handed him the coffee. "Here. You need it more than I do." She wished there was more she could do to make him feel better.

"Thanks." He slumped back down in the driver's seat. "I know what you're trying to do, and I appreciate it."

"Is it working?" she asked softly.

He made a face at her over the top of his coffee mug. "Eh, maybe you should kiss me again to be sure."

She chuckled. "If I do, we're never going to make it to our first search and rescue training session."

He wrinkled his nose at her. "I see where your priorities are."

She reached over to squeeze his forearm, which he flexed for her benefit. "I just want you to be okay."

He was still for a moment before answering. "I'm always okay when I'm with you, Reese."

"Garek," she sighed. "Sometimes you say the sweetest things." Then she added in a teasing voice,

"Almost like you're buttering me up, because you want something from me."

"I do want something from you." Their gazes met and held.

It was suddenly harder for her to breathe.

"It's something we're going to have to talk about eventually, Reese." His voice was husky with a longing that tugged every heartstring in her.

She glanced away first. "I know." A wave of dizziness swept her, making her long for a pair of emotional brakes to tap. Ever since their first kiss, things had been speeding along in their relationship so quickly — almost too quickly. However, she knew he was right. They needed to talk about where things were heading between them. "We will. Soon."

His expression brightened. "But first we have a dog training session to attend." He threw the vehicle into reverse, still sipping on his coffee.

THE BASEMENT TRAINING area at the Heart Lake Police Department was full of men and dogs when they arrived. Shep glanced up and gave Reese a wide grin as she sauntered through the door with Chips on a leash. Well, that was her intent, anyway. Chips took one look at the occupants of the room and more or less dragged Reese along as she flew to greet her former foster parent.

"Whoa, Chips!" she squealed. "Whoa there, puppy!"

The room dissolved into male laughter.

"She's not a runaway horse, you know." Shep rose from his crouch over the pair of German Shepherds he'd been harnessing. "Instead of giddy-up and whoa, try telling her to sit and stay."

The tall blonde police officer Chips had been trying to reach straightened and held out a hand to her. "I'm Lincoln Hudson. It's nice to finally meet you, Miss Summerville."

"Reese. Just Reese," she corrected dryly as she shook his hand. "Survivalist and thrill-seeker extraordinaire." She figured she might as well own up to what everyone else in the room was thinking. "I may never be an expert search and rescuer like the rest of you, but I'd really like to help out if you don't mind giving me a few pointers." She grimaced. "It may not seem like it, but that's kind of the whole point of my show — teaching extreme athletes how to do things better and safer. I mean, it's not like we're going to stop them from going out there and doing their crazy stuff."

"Very good point." An auburn-haired deputy smirked knowingly in Shep's direction as he swaggered across the room to shake her hand. "I'm Wheeler Remington, the voice of reason."

His words were met with loud guffaws from his fellow deputies.

"Hey!" He spun around to face them, hands in the air. "I'm not the one auditioning to bungee jump my way across an icy canyon."

Shep shrugged. "It's okay if you want to play it safe back in the office, mate, but don't knock it if you haven't tried it."

"Hold on a sec!" Looking alarmed, Lincoln Hudson stepped into the middle of the room with Glory on a leash to face Shep. The Golden Retriever gave an excited yip as she perceived they were now the center of attention. "You're actually serious about being on the Max West Adventures show?"

"I am." Shep scowled. "I was thinking a local guy might stand a decent chance of going for the gold against a bunch of city-slickers. I grew up in these mountains, you know."

"Alright, alright." Shaking his head in amazement, Lincoln whistled for the dogs to quiet down. "Guess we better double down on our training, seeing as how we're about to have one of our own out there on the slopes."

He signaled to Wheeler. "Let's pull out the bite sleeves and review a few of the basics for Reese and Garek's benefit."

He proceeded to lead them in a series of exercises that entailed giving their dogs the order to attack. One by one, the dogs launched themselves at their owners, snapping and snarling as they latched on to the bite sleeves covering their arms.

"We don't spend a lot of time on the offensive like this," Lincoln explained with a grin. "That's more for big city patrols and such, but it's a great bonding exercise with your dogs. It helps the two of you learn to trust each other."

After Reese went through several rounds of the bite exercise, she removed her sleeve, puffing from exertion. "I don't ever want to be on this beautiful girl's bad side." She bent to give Chips a few milk bone snacks as a reward. "She could do some serious damage if properly provoked."

"It's true." Lincoln's expression grew serious. "Back at the Texas Hotline Training Center, they often referred to our dogs as loaded weapons. Our urban warfare instructor told us to train hard and aim them carefully."

Reese glanced over at Garek as he gave Fish a small handful of snacks from the jar the PD had provided for their training session. "So, ah...my business partner has some tracking and scenting experience due to his volunteer work at the fire department. However, I don't, and that's what I need the most. One of our biggest concerns during our winter challenge is going to be lost hikers."

Garek's gaze was warm with approval and something else. She could tell he appreciated her referring to him to as her business partner in front of others.

"She's right," he chimed in. "Most of this season's contestants are mountain climbers and extreme skiers, but only one of them has prior military service. He probably won't put on as big of a show for the cameras, but I'd vouch for his land navigation skills over theirs any day." He straightened and slung an arm possessively around her shoulders. "Like Reese said, lost hikers are going to be our biggest risk. They're fine when the weather's good, but stir up an unexpected snowstorm, and the amateur ones get disoriented pretty quickly."

She leaned closer to him, liking the weight of his arm around her.

Shep frowned as he glanced between the two of them. "I'd say my tracking skills are well above average. More like the expert category."

"In your not-so-humble opinion," Wheeler muttered beneath his breath as he circled the room to collect their bite sleeves.

Shep popped his younger co-worker with a swift punch to the shoulder.

Garek nodded, drumming his fingers idly against Reese's upper arm. "If you get selected to compete, sounds like we'll have two contestants whose land nav skills I can safely vouch for. That's still only two out of twelve, though. That's why we're here, soaking up all the training we can get."

"If I get selected," Shep scoffed, latching on to that one word. "If?" He rolled his eyes at Reese. "Should we tell him now, hon, or would that spoil the surprise?"

She feigned a chuckle at his words, though she hated the way Garek's tall frame stiffened at the careless endearment Shep had thrown her way. "How about we surprise him?" she suggested brightly.

If Shep was half the skier in the snow that he was on the water, their viewers were in for a real treat — *when*, not if, he made the show.

CHAPTER 6: SHOW TRYOUTS

GAREK

Garek and Reese started off the next morning in the same basement room of the police station. Both Shep and Wheeler were in attendance again today. This time, Lincoln had an obstacle course set up, consisting of plastic bowls filled with specimens. The idea was to train Fish and Chips to follow the trail of a specific scent from bowl to bowl — ignoring the bowls that contained the wrong scent and only continuing along the path of bowls that contained the right scent. It was an easy exercise that both dogs got the hang of pretty quickly.

"Let's try something more challenging," Lincoln announced near the end of the training session. He beckoned to Garek. "Since you've done this before, how about you help me set up the next course? I'm gonna need your shirt, hat, and anything else you can lend to the cause. That way Reese and Chips have a live target to hunt down."

Garek eagerly shrugged out of his gray hoodie, not minding the fact that he was wearing a chest-hugging white t-shirt underneath. He did plenty of flexing for Reese's benefit as he handed over the requested items.

She watched him with an interested sparkle in her blue gaze and a tinge of pink on her cheeks. He hoped it meant she was remembering the number of times she'd been in his arms during the last couple of days, because he was having a difficult time thinking of anything else.

It annoyed him the way Shep elbowed his way between him and Reese to help her adjust something on Chips' leash. Garek seriously doubted the gesture had any real point to it, other than getting close to her. He held his cool — just barely — even when Shep reached up to adjust Reese's hold on the leash.

"Hold her like this," he instructed. "Gotta show her who's boss."

At the mention of the word boss, Reese glanced Garek's way and blushed.

Shep must have misunderstood the reason for the color in her cheeks. "And now for a round of Marco Polo." He lightly squeezed Reese's shoulder before he stepped back.

Visions of breaking the man's hand mentally floated in front of Garek's eyes. It took him a second to get a grip. Once his anger was firmly back in check, he mentally vowed not to go easy on the guy during the coming tryouts.

"Clock's ticking. We need to hurry." Lincoln created a trail out of Garek's clothing items, dragging a few of them along the floor to spread his scent to key locations around the training area. "You." He pointed at Garek. "We need you out of sight on the other side of the door at the end of the course. That'll force Chips to use her scent abilities only for this exercise, not her sight."

Garek nodded and jogged for the exit. He could only hope and pray that Shep didn't try anything with Reese in his absence that would result in fisticuffs upon his return. She'd insisted she had no plans to encourage the guy's interest. However, Shep didn't seem to require much encouragement. He was in to her, no doubt about it.

On the other side of the door, Garek folded his arms and leaned back against the wall with a huff of frustration. If he was being honest with himself, his current stress level was mostly his fault. He was the one who'd spent the last few years dragging his heels with Reese for one reason or another. Yeah, it was true he'd been trying to give her the time and space she needed to grieve, but it was equally true that he'd been worried senseless about his dad's less than stellar traits manifesting themselves in him. However, the biggest reason he'd held back asking her on a date was out of stinking, rotten cowardice. He'd been too afraid of ruining their friendship, too afraid of losing her for good.

She was so important to him, so vital to his personal happiness, that he'd convinced himself he'd rather have her as a friend than to not have her in his life at all. Unfortunately, it had taken Shep Whitaker about five seconds during Garek's first encounter with him to show him just how stupid he'd been acting. By failing to ask Reese out sooner, Garek was running the very real risk of having some other man swoop in and snap her up from him.

Over my dead body! Fury pushed Garek off the wall and made him swivel toward the open doorway. If Shep so much as tried to—

"Gotcha!" Reese's voice sang out.

In the same moment, fifty pounds of fur and canine muscle slammed into Garek's chest.

Oof! His breath came out in an ungallant huff as he absorbed the impact. "Yep," he wheezed, kissing her with his eyes. "You've got me, darling." He enjoyed dragging another blush out of her, not caring who overheard their exchange.

He allowed his shoulder to brush hers as they re-entered the training room together.

"Nice job!" Shep strode their way to give her a high-five. He leaned in for a quick hug before stepping back.

To Garek's unholy delight, Chips gave a growl of warning.

"He's a friend," Reese protested, wagging a finger in gentle admonition at the dog.

Garek was tempted to reward the animal with a snack when no one was looking. However, he resisted the temptation. They were no longer in junior high, and he doubted Reese would be impressed if he trained Chips to bite the guy.

It was hard, but he resisted the temptation to indulge in such an immature prank. Instead, he shrugged back into his hoodie and slapped on his ball cap. Then he helped her load the dogs into the back of the Land Rover.

"We get to keep them, right?" Her voice was pleading as she latched Chips' cage closed and met Garek's questioning gaze.

"You mean the dogs?" In his head, he was still strangling Shep in six different directions.

"Yes, pretty please with sprinkles on top."

He spread his hands. "Lincoln never really said, but—"

"Yes, Reese." Lincoln jogged past them on his way to the police cruiser that was parked in the spot next to theirs. "The answer to your question is a thousand yeses with my wife's undying gratitude." He propped one boot on the running board of his car and leaned his forearms on the window. "Katie has already threatened to move me out to the porch if I bring another mutt home."

"So if we keep Fish and Chips, we're basically saving your marriage," Reese joked, looking over-joyed at the news.

"Bingo!" He jabbed a finger in the air at her. "If you want, we can talk official adoption papers when I get back from this call."

She nodded happily. "We're heading to the arena to start our last set of tryouts. You can meet us there, or we can meet you back here — whatever works best for everyone."

"Lemme get back with you on that." He gave her a thumbs up and slid behind the wheel. Rolling across the parking lot, he switched on his flashers. Only after he pulled onto the highway did he turn on his police siren.

Fish and Chips howled in unison with the wail of his siren until he drove out of earshot.

GAREK KNEW Reese had chosen the arena for their tryouts for all the usual reasons — plenty of space, good lighting, and the sense it would give every candidate of being on public display. First and foremost, Max West Adventures was a reality show. Providing top-rated entertainment value to their viewers was crucial to keeping the generosity of their sponsors pouring in.

Matt and Carl McGraw had finally made it into town mid-day yesterday with their silver bullet fifth wheel they lived in. Their flashy Dodge Ram with its extra wide tires was spattered with so much mud that Garek was sure they'd taken a detour on their way to Heart Lake. The two brothers were forever off-roading on some adventure or another with either their truck or the dirt bikes they kept stowed in the rear compartment of their trailer.

Matt headed his way across the arena with his arms stretched wide and his freckled face beaming. His slouched leather Stetson was pushed back a few inches. "What do you think of the tryout course?" he crowed. "Not bad for something we had to slap together last-minute, eh?"

Garek dragged a hand across the stubble on his chin as he surveyed their work. Matt wasn't exaggerating. Their crew all too frequently had to push against impossible deadlines to build their sets and get their camera gear in place. Today was no exception. However, Matt and Carl had managed to outdo themselves yet again.

With the help of a snow-blowing machine Reese had rented from a nearby ski resort, they'd transformed the arena into a triple set of tryout lanes that were truly camera worthy. The brothers had started off the course with a snow-packed hill that swooped

a good twenty feet downward. Each lane was separated by a set of multi-colored pennant flags — red,
yellow, and orange — that were easy to pick out
against their snowy white backdrop.

After a short straight-of-way, the lanes were
punctuated by a series of jumps with gradually
increasing heights. Next, the lanes widened into a
set of curves and obstacles. As the lanes worked
their way around the oval arena, they ended in
different places to accommodate the extra distance
added to the outer lanes by the curves. If the candidate wished to rack up a few bonus points, they
could push onward free-style for another thirty
yards or so.

"Come on, man!" Matt gave a small whoop of
impatience. "Lay it on me. What do you like about it,
and what are you gonna make us change?"

Garek pointed at the first slope. "Did you and
Carl do a test run yet?"

"Is the sky blue?" Matt sighed. "Of course we
did. Twice. Carl wanted to run our bikes through it
afterward, but there wouldn't have been enough time
to repack the snow." He let out a long-suffering sigh.
"So we're holding off on that until the tear-down."

Garek held out a fist, already picturing the two
wild-haired brothers gunning it through the arena on
their dirt bikes. "I don't see any changes needed."

"Really?" Looking surprised, Matt obliged him
with a fist-bump. "Carl figured you'd want us to add

a few more rails on the free-style stretch, like you usually do."

Garek shook his head. "Nah. Let's hold off this time. Reese said she'd like to get started within the hour, and it takes time to anchor down and test anything extra."

"We work fast. You know that."

"I'll check with her real quick, but I'm thinking the answer's still gonna be no. I think it looks good as-is."

"You're the boss." As Matt jogged away, Garek heard him grumble, "Prob'ly could've slept in another half hour at least."

Reese agreed with Garek's call. "Yes, let's leave the course as-is, so we can start on time. Shep needs to get back to the station as soon as possible. Sounds like they're being overrun with calls this morning."

Since Shep hadn't yet made his appearance in the arena, Garek could only presume he'd texted her.

Great. On top of being the world's biggest flirt, Shep had Reese's phone number. *My day just keeps getting better.* Garek shook his head at the woman of his dreams.

"What?" she demanded.

"Nothing," he sighed. He started to stride past her. On a whim, however, he paused. Leaning her way, he tipped her chin up and planted a hard kiss on her mouth.

Her lips parted in astonishment. "That didn't feel like nothing," she hissed.

"I agree." Whistling, he continued on his way to the metal platform where he and Reese would be observing and critiquing each candidate.

In the end, a total of eleven locals showed up to try out for the final slot on the Max West Adventures show. It was a larger number than they'd been expecting.

"I guess our advertising worked," Reese mused as she scanned each application. Unfortunately, she and Garek had to eliminate two candidates right up front for medically disqualifying reasons. One had come down with a migraine that was making him overly sensitive to sunlight, and the other was wearing a plaster cast on his arm.

"I'm as disappointed as you are," she informed each man regretfully, "but your safety is more important to us than anything else. Thanks so much for applying. We truly appreciate your support of Max West Adventures." As a consolation offering, she loaded the two guys down with licensed t-shirts and hoodies, sports bottles, and signed posters. They left happy.

"That leaves us with three rounds of candidates. I'm putting Shep on the first one, so he can scoot back to the station right afterward."

"Oh, is he here already? I didn't see him." Garek glanced around at the sparsely filled silver bleachers.

"Seriously? How could you possibly miss that?" She pointed toward the growing huddle of people around what he'd presumed to be a restaurant vendor. Or a mascot. Or a complete moron.

"You've got to be kidding me!" His gaze narrowed on the object of his irritation. The guy was wearing a white-feathered chicken costume with a floppy red crest on top of his head.

"That's a country boy for you." Reese shook her head, grinning. "Wheeler probably dared him to do it. There might even be bets riding on it back at the station."

Garek shook his head. "That's not distracting at all. Can he even ski in that thing?"

"You tell me." Reese chuckled as she motioned for the first three contestants to take their places at the starting line. She held her pop gun in the air and allowed the anticipation in the arena to build.

Unlike the live show, there was no official judging panel for the tryouts. Reese and Garek had their own top-secret method for weeding through the candidates and choosing the perfect athletes for their show. It was part of the gig. Everyone knew it, and most people accepted it without too much fuss.

They'd discovered their growing audience preferred a diverse cast in terms of ages, backgrounds, and skill levels. It wasn't the Olympics, so none of the candidates were expected to be professional athletes, though many were. The viewers of their show especially adored watching Reese and Garek pit an underdog or two against the higher skilled contestants.

Or, in this case, a chicken. Garek watched Shep take his place amidst the snickers of his viewers. The guy played up the costume every step of the way, even popping a squat to lay an imaginary egg at the top of the hill. Their growing audience howled with mirth from the stands.

Reese's pop gun went off, and the three skiers shot down the hill. One of them resembled a feathery white bullet with a blur of red on his head. Shep quickly took the lead. Despite the flips he did at the end of the two tallest jumps, he kept the lead.

Yeah, the guy could ski. With a burst of grudging admiration, Garek watched as Shep continued his antics along the free-style stretch. Since the timed portion was over, he skied backwards and ended up stumbling against the first rail. Or pretended to... Instead of falling, however, he hopped on top of it and skied backwards down it. All the bumbling and bobbling was apparently part of his act.

The audience laughed, clapped, and shrieked at the tops of their lungs for him. Garek shook his head at Reese. Bending close to her earlobe, he inquired, "Do we have to even watch the others?" Though he was less than thrilled about the fact, he knew they had their twelfth candidate in their sights already.

"You know we do." She spared him a warm smile. "It's only fair."

Or the appearance of being fair, at least. "The others have to know they don't stand a chance of competing with that clown."

"They probably do, but keeping them in suspense until our final announcement is half the fun. Let 'em have their two minutes of fame."

She and Garek were barely watching the second round of contestants, however, as Shep skied in their direction. He flapped his arms and bawked like a chicken beneath their platform.

Reese bent down and snatched up a handful of snow to form into a ball. She sent it crashing off the top of his head, making his red crest flap in the opposite direction.

He neither ducked nor flinched. "So did I pass the test, beautiful?"

Garek was tempted to ball up another snowball and zing it straight into his smug face. The guy had to have witnessed their kiss from earlier, but it didn't seem to be dampening his flirtatious tendencies one bit.

She chuckled. "You'll have to wait for the official announcement, same as everyone else."

He pretended to scowl ferociously at her. "Guess I better go save lives while you and your business partner continue to put them in jeopardy." He made the words *business partner* sound like they were chicken fried and dripping with sarcasm.

She chuckled again and glanced over at Garek. "Should we give him a down feather sized hint of our decision?"

He shrugged offhandedly. "Probably wouldn't hurt to let him know all twelve of our final contestants will be invited to preview the official course tomorrow. Ten o'clock sharp." Garek winked at her. "That way he can pencil it in, just in case."

She spread her hands as she met Shep's questioning gaze. "You heard my partner. Think you can be here at ten o'clock?"

He waggled his brows at her. "I reckon, so long as no one robs a bank on my way here."

Garek watched the cocky police officer swagger off, shaking his tail-feathers every few steps, and wasn't at all happy to know that Reese would be watching *that* over the next few days.

A guy who, most unfortunately, was as determined as Garek to date her.

CHAPTER 7: SNOWBOUND

GAREK

Garek awoke to the sound of snow and sleet slapping against the windows of the apartment over the garage. "That's just great," he muttered, rolling out of bed. It looked as if the weather was going to make today's dry run with the Max West Adventures contestants a little more exciting than they'd originally planned.

By the time he tossed on his thermal shirt and leggings beneath his ski pants, the sound of the wind had escalated to a full howl. Pulling a plaid shirt over his thermals, he clapped on an insulated cap with earflaps and reached for his boots. Though he hadn't yet checked the weather forecast, he was already mentally forming his arguments to Reese for why they should postpone this morning's tour of the course. Maybe they could squeeze it in later in the day after the snow let up.

Worst-case scenario, they would have to post-pone the filming of their opening episode by a few hours or days. The delay was unfortunate, but they always put the safety of their contestants first.

"Better safe than sorry," Garek muttered beneath his breath. He tugged on his coat and gloves and tromped his way across the snow-caked driveway to the back porch of the mill house.

The moon was forming a bluish-white glow behind the sleet and snow. It was too early for the first rays of sun to light up the horizon, not that they would generate more than a distant haze in this storm. *Shoot!* Garek was having trouble seeing more than three to five feet in front of him.

Though it was a few minutes shy of five o'clock, he found the kitchen windows were already aglow as he mounted the porch steps. He stomped his way across the planks to loosen the snow caked to his boot treads.

Reese met him at the door. "Good golly!" She shivered. "I was wondering if you were going to skip our coffee date and wait it out over the garage."

Liking that she'd called their new morning ritual a date, he shook the snow from his coat before stepping inside and shutting the door behind him.

Reese was coatless and shivering in a hot pink sweatshirt, with her slender arms wrapped around her middle.

Grinning in appreciation at the sight of her,

Garek tossed his coat around her shoulders.

"Thanks." She snuggled gratefully into it and pulled the flaps more tightly around her, as if trying to absorb all final traces of his body heat.

"What are best friends for?" He gave a playful tap to her upturned nose. The backs of his fingers brushed against her lips as he returned his hand to his side.

Her mouth parted in surprise, cheekbones turning rosy.

"It's alright. You don't have to answer that." He had to clear his throat to get rid of the huskiness. Man, but she was beautiful in the morning!

"Maybe I want to. You did say we needed to talk about our friendship," she pointed out shyly. "Eventually."

His heart pounded in anticipation of hearing her thoughts on the subject. "Is that what time of day it is?" he teased. "Eventually?"

She waved at the windows that were clicking from the tiny balls of sleet and ice hitting them. "I'm going to go with yes, seeing as how we're about to experience a delayed start to today's regularly sched-uled program."

"A fireside chat it is," he returned cheerfully. "Preferably with coffee," he added, sniffing the air.

"I'm one step ahead of you, partner." She stepped sassily around him to scoop up two thermos mugs from the granite countertop. "Pure black with no cream or sugar. Just the way you like it." She pressed one of the mugs into his hands with a grimace. "I don't know how you pour straight petroleum down your throat like that."

He reached over to lightly pinch her chin. "Doesn't mean I don't enjoy a splash of vanilla cream with my mornings now and then."

She blushed as the double meaning of his words sank in. "So, ah..." She sounded so nervous that he almost spun her around, right then and there, to plant a kiss on her.

Instead, he followed her into the great room where she had a fire leaping in the hearth. He nudged the nearest leather loveseat a few inches closer to the fire before waving her into it.

As he took a seat beside her, he hooked an arm around her shoulders and drew her against his side.

Her blue gaze met his, clouded with confusion.

He dipped his head closer. "I think it's time to prove to you that your more refined palate can handle a bit of straight black brew, as well." Thoroughly intoxicated by her scent and nearness, he tipped his forehead against hers to nuzzle the edge of her mouth.

"Garek," she whispered.

"Right here, baby." He dragged his lips gently over hers, reveling in their warm, velvety softness.

Most unfortunately, the jangle of a cell phone shattered the moment.

"I'm so sorry!" Yanking her phone from the pocket of her jeans, Reese held it to her ear. "Max West Adventures. Reese Summerville speaking," she announced in a breathless voice.

Though the room was lit by nothing more than the flicker of fire light, Garek could see her features pale.

"What do you mean, they went out ahead of schedule?" She paused. "Are you sure?" she grated out. Then she exclaimed, "Oh, my lands, yes! We'll divide and conquer. You and Carl call the first half of the list. Garek and I will call the second half. Tell everyone that the coordinates were wrong and that we'll send the correct ones in a bit." She paused again. "Of course, we're lying to them, so you better use your most convincing voice. We can't afford to have them venture out in this weather."

She ended the call and stared in alarm at Garek. "This could be bad!"

He traced the lower half of her cheek with his thumb. "What's going on, darling?"

She whooshed out a breath. "According to Matt, there was a glitch with our email server and the coordinates to our ski course were sent a few hours early to the contestants."

Garek frowned. "Meaning all twelve of our candidates are in possession of them right now?"

"Right now," she affirmed grimly. "So we better start calling them. You take contestant six, and I'll take contestant seven. Like you just heard me explain to Matt, we need to inform everyone that the coordinates are wrong. Tell them we're in the process of sending out the correct ones and to stand down until they receive them."

They spent the next ten minutes on the phone, reaching out to each contestant. Then they rang Matt again.

"Okay. We reached all of ours," Reese reported to him in relief. "What's the skinny on your half of the list?"

"The only one we couldn't reach was Number Five." Matt sounded a little worried. "Harper Croft from New Jersey. Carl is headed to her hotel now to check on her in person."

Reese momentarily squeezed her eyelids shut. "Are you trying to tell me he took his dirt bike out in this weather?"

"Nope. He wore his snow shoes," Matt returned cheerfully.

"Lord, give me strength," she moaned, opening her eyes to meet Garek's questioning gaze. "Say it isn't so."

"He's in his heated suit and GPS goggles," Matt informed her loftily. "He'll be fine."

"How many times have I tried to tell you we're not Power Rangers?" she sighed.

"It's less than two miles away," Matt continued as if he hadn't heard her. "Carl will be at the hotel in twenty minutes tops. Then you can quit your mother hen fretting over nothing."

"I would love to quit worrying," she informed him in a shaky voice. "I'm not so sure that's going to be the outcome, though." She shot Garek a worried look. "Listen, Matt. I'm going to get off the line for a few minutes, but—"

"Yeah, yeah. I'll call you back the moment I hear from him," he promised.

"Thanks, Matt." She ended the call, looking a tad dizzy.

"What do we know about Number Five?" Garek asked quickly.

Reese smoothed a hand over the loose strands escaping from her ponytail. "As you already know, she's our underdog."

"But?" he prodded, sensing there was more to the story.

"She has a sister in the advanced stages of bone cancer."

"Poor kid!" He nodded. "I remember that from her application."

"There's more." She pressed a hand to her stomach as if it pained her. "Yesterday, I overheard her talking to another candidate about some cutting edge treatments she'd like her sister to try next. I'm not sure about the details other than it's in Europe, it's expensive, and it's not going to be covered by any insurance."

"Sorry to hear it." Garek's chest twisted at the news, though he wasn't surprised about the expense. Cancer treatments cost an arm and a leg.

"She sounded desperate, Garek. And you know how that old saying goes — desperate people do desperate things."

"Like head out in a blizzard to scope out a ski course ahead of the competition," he finished glumly.

"Exactly."

"Let's not jump to any conclusions yet," he cautioned. "There's a bunch of other reasons why Harper Croft might not have answered her phone. It might be turned off, or she might have lost it. She might even be in the shower for all we know."

As it turned out, none of those things were true. Matt rang them in exactly twenty-two minutes and thirty-five seconds. "She's gone," he reported hoarsely.

"Gone?" Reese squeaked. "Details, details!"

"Yep. Carl posed as her husband at the front desk and somehow convinced them to give him a keycard to her room. She's gone, as in gone. Skis and poles are missing. No coat or other gear in her closet. All that's left is a half-empty suitcase and a picture of her with some woman who looks enough like her to be her twin."

"Twins!" Reese groaned, covering her face with a hand. "This is even worse than I realized."

"Does this mean we need to go after her?" Matt

asked excitedly. "I can see the headlines now. Dare-devil brothers launch a risky mountain rescue op—"

"Absolutely not!" Reese shouted, lowering her hand. "This is a job for the Heart Lake Police Department's Search and Rescue Team. You tell Carl to stay at the hotel. He can get a room and order room service. I don't care. I'll cover the bill. Just tell him to stay put until the storm dies down."

"Yes, ma'am," Matt returned in a more subdued voice.

"I mean it, Matt."

"Yep. Room service. Got it," he said flatly and disconnected the line.

Reese and Garek spent the next several minutes on the phone with Officer Lincoln Hudson, discussing the pros and cons of launching a rescue operation.

"We can't send our chopper out in this mess," he warned. "The visibility is way too poor right now. The dogs won't be able to do much in the way of scenting and tracking, either, until the worst of it dies down."

"You mean we're supposed to just sit here and do nothing?" Reese demanded shrilly.

"I know that sounds every shade of wrong and rotten, but yes. That's exactly what we need to do right now. We'll get out there as soon as it's safe to," he advised calmly.

"Oh, Lincoln," she sighed.

"We're no good to anyone if we're just as lost as they are," he pointed out.

"I know, but—"

"Or catching our death of hypothermia."

"I hear you, but—"

"I'm trained and certified in this stuff," he assured. "You're just going to have to trust me, okay?"

"Okay," she muttered darkly. Garek could tell she wasn't convinced, though.

"Keep your phones on, you two," Lincoln continued. "This storm could blow over in minutes or even seconds. We'll launch a rescue attempt at the earliest possible opportunity. I promise."

"Thanks." Reese ended the call with a haunted look. "Garek," she murmured in a broken voice. "The poor woman's twin sister is dying of cancer. We can't just leave her out there alone."

"You heard Lincoln. Rushing into the eye of a storm won't help anyone."

Reese gave a low moan of despair. She dropped her phone in her lap and covered her face with both hands. "This feels like my mother's boat crash all over again. We're just sitting here, waiting for the other shoe to drop."

"Don't go there," he crooned, gathering her close. He tucked her head beneath his chin and held her tightly, trying to will away her fears.

"Too late." She drew a shuddery breath. "I'm already there."

"We're going to go after Harper as soon as it's safe to."

"What if she can't hold on that long?"

"You don't know that, Reese. Have a little faith."

"I'm trying to, Garek. I really am. But my heart is telling me this isn't the time to sit and wait. If it was you or me out there..."

"It's not, sweetheart." He was eternally grateful that it wasn't.

"But if it was me," she pressed. "Would you do something besides wait?"

"That's not a fair question, baby." When it came to anything involving Reese, all of his rationale flew out the window. She knew that.

"All I'm trying to say is maybe we should be giving this poor woman's situation the same sense of urgency."

"You heard what Lincoln said," Garek reminded in a quiet voice against her temple. He couldn't stand the thought of Reese going out in this weather, even if he went with her.

"I did." She yanked her head up, looking troubled. "I also heard what he didn't say. In the time it takes for this storm to die down, Contestant Number Five could die out there — for no other crime than being a little over zealous about paying for her sister's medical treatments." Reese shook her head vehemently. "I couldn't save my mother, Garek, and maybe everyone was right. Maybe it wasn't in my power back then, but this is. I'm here in Heart Lake, probably no more than a mile or two from Harper Croft's current location."

He watched, perplexed, as she leaped to her feet.

"I'm going after her, Garek. I have to, or I'll never be able to live with myself again."

Reese spoke with such a deep conviction that he knew there would be no talking her out of it. Rising from the loveseat, he faced her squarely. "I'm going with you."

Her eyes grew damp. "I'm not asking you to."

His jaw grew hard. "You don't need to. As strongly as you feel about locating our missing contestant, multiply it by a hundred thousand, and you might come close to how I feel about not letting you go out there alone."

She gave him a tremulous smile. "I said it before. You're a good man, Garek. The best there is." She mumbled her way through the checklist they would need to launch their expedition. "We'll wear our heated suits, supply packs, and GPS goggles."

As a precaution, Garek additionally shot off a short text to Lincoln Hudson as he and Reese left the mill house. There was no way he was venturing out into the storm without notifying someone else what they were up to.

Lincoln's response was immediate: *Abort the mission! That's an order, my friends.*

Unfortunately, he wasn't in any position to give

them orders, and he knew it.

Garek texted back: *I'll keep sending coordinates as long as our phone service lasts*. It was the best he could do.

He and Reese set out in their snow shoes with their skis strapped to their backs and their poles in hand. For the next hour, they battled their way against the storm toward the line of mountains towering over Heart Lake.

The first glow of sunrise finally crept over the horizon, making it easier to see, but just barely. For a few minutes, it seemed as if the storm might be abating. Then the winds picked up, and the snow started falling thicker than before.

Garek reached for Reese and hooked a bungee cord to the belt of her coat.

"Thanks!" she shouted to him over the gale.

He squeezed her hand in response.

The snow in their path drifted higher, making it harder and harder to press forward despite the aid of their snow shoes. In his gut, Garek knew they should probably seek shelter and wait out the storm — just like Lincoln had advised. However, Reese pressed doggedly on toward their test run coordinates, and he followed. They reached the base of the mountains and dug in their ski poles to continue onward and upward.

Ten minutes or so into their mountainous trek, an ominous *whump* filled their ears. Though Garek had never experienced such a thing in real life, he'd watched it all too many times on extreme sports videos. Dread speared his gut as he recognized the sound of the snow shifting over their heads. Unless he was mistaken, it was the start of an avalanche higher up on the mountain.

He anxiously scanned their surroundings for shelter, but it was still too difficult to see more than a few feet ahead of them. Since the sound seemed to be coming from the east, he grabbed Reese's gloved hand and started jogging west.

Her head whipped his way in surprise, but she didn't fight him as he ran sideways across the mountain with every last ounce of strength in him. They didn't move nearly as quickly as he would've liked. By some miracle, however, they managed to outrun all but the outer edges of the deadly river of snow. They stumbled through its over-spray, coughing and gagging, and continued running until they were out of breath.

Whirling around, they watched in fascination as the white rivulets of snow continued on down the side of the mountain, covering everything in its path. Enormous spruces and pines that once stretched eighty feet or more toward the sky were buried a good halfway up their stalwart trunks.

By now, Garek and Reese were so thoroughly coated in snow that they resembled two abominable snowmen. He had to swipe his fingers like windshield wipers across the lenses of his goggles to see her. That's when he realized she was having difficulty standing.

He released her hand to slide an arm around her waist. She sagged gratefully against him. "What happened?" he hollered against the driving wind.

"It's my ankle," she hollered back.

Muttering a prayer for strength, he had to half drag and half carry her as they continued on. He lost track of the time as they trudged in what he hoped was a direct line back toward the lake. It might have been minutes or even an hour before the sharp edges of a roofline drew into view.

To his disappointment, it wasn't the edge of town — not even close; but it was shelter. He eyed the weathered cabin, hoping it contained a fireplace.

It did, along with a stack of firewood in a box beside the hearth. Though it was unlocked and empty of occupants, it ended up being well-stocked with blankets and can goods. It was a lucky find in the middle of nowhere, possibly someone's hunting cabin. Though Garek and Reese were trespassing, it felt like nothing short of a miracle to be under a roof again.

He deposited her on a rug in front of the hearth, yanked off his goggles, and got a fire started. It took a while for the two of them to thaw out enough to carry on a conversation.

Reese's expression crumpled as she slid off her

goggles. "We tried, but failed." She shivered in misery, her eyes filling with tears. "We're in here where it's safe, and Harper Croft is still out there somewhere, alone and cold."

He silently helped her unzip her coat and open the flaps toward the fire.

"I really thought this would work," she whispered brokenly. "We had the coordinates and all the right equipment."

"There's no way you could've predicted an avalanche, sweetheart." He knelt on the rug beside her.

"It still feels like a failure," she rasped.

"Come here, you." He held out his arms to her.

After a moment of hesitation, she leaned into him.

"What are we going to do, Garek?" She cuddled closer.

"We're going to wrap that swollen ankle of yours, stay warm, and pray that Number Five makes it." It probably wasn't what Reese wanted to hear, but that was all the wisdom he possessed at the moment. "Call me a lunatic, but I still believe in Christmas miracles, darling," he added in a lighter voice. "Do you?"

"I do now."

To his shock, she grabbed two fistfuls of his shirt to tug him closer. "I know things are bad right now, but I just realized something very, very important."

"I'm listening, darling."

She gazed at him with her heart in her eyes. "The only reason any man would follow any woman into a storm like this is out of crazy, stupid love."

"Yeah." He couldn't have said it better himself.

"That's what you've been trying to tell me the past few days, isn't it? You love me, Garek Borden." She scanned his features in awe. "You really, really love me."

"With everything in me." He tenderly cupped her face with both hands, marveling at the realization she was finally his — all his. Though her cheeks were wind-chapped, she had never been more beautiful to him. He would never get tired of looking at her, never get tired of being with her. He wanted to share all of her good times and all of her bad times while they lived and loved and grew old together.

"I love you, too." Tears welled in her eyes and streaked down her cheeks. He could tell they were happy ones, since he'd witnessed every kind of tears Reese Summerville had shed in the past twenty-something years. "I love you so much, Garek. I think..." her voice hitched over a sob, "I always have."

The wind was still screaming on the other side of the cabin windows, but it no longer mattered. It felt like he'd waited a lifetime to hear those words. His lips found hers, and the storm outside disappeared as the storm inside their hearts took over.

CHAPTER 8: ICY VENTURE

REESE

Reese winced as Garek wrapped her ankle in a thick roll of gauze. Then a giggle escaped her as his fingertips brushed the ball of her foot.

"Ticklish?" A wicked shade of interest lit his dark features.

She carefully evaded his probing gaze. "I'd rather not talk about it."

"I see. Note to self," he returned silkily. "The woman I love has ticklish feet. Never know when that kind of information might prove useful."

"You're a truly awful person," she informed him with a dramatic sigh.

"No, I'm pretty sure you said I was a good man. The best there is."

"It's one of the many shortcomings of the English

language." She waved a hand in mock dismissal of his words. "So much gets lost in context."

"Is that so?" he demanded, his brown eyes glinting with humor.

"Most unfortunately." She pouted for good measure.

"Well, here's some context for you, Miss Summerville." He swooped in to nip a light trail of kisses from her chin to her earlobe. "Now that we're snowbound together in this cabin, I don't mind telling you the real reason I accepted your invitation to accompany you to Heart Lake."

"Oo!" She leaned away from him so she could shoot a hand into the air like a school kid. "I think I know the answer to this one."

"You think?"

"Yep. You were hoping for a white Christmas and were worried that sunny Dallas might not deliver it." She batted her lashes at him.

"Nobody in their right mind wants this much white stuff for Christmas." He gestured ruefully at the cabin's snow-caked windows.

"Okay, I give up. What's your super secret reason for coming to Heart Lake?"

"The fact that every inch of my heart belongs to you." He slid his arms around her and gathered her close again. "I didn't want that other job opportunity to be the fork in the road that took us in two different directions. My biggest plan for the future is to be with you, darling. It always has been."

"Wow! That's some pretty incredible context," she murmured, swaying closer.

"Glad you think so because I'm just getting started." He dipped his head over hers, a world of promises burning in his gaze.

The buzzing of a cell phone made him pause before his lips touched hers.

"The man's timing is impeccable." He grimaced as he pulled his phone from the pocket of his ski pants.

"Who's timing?" It sounded as if he'd been expecting the call, which utterly mystified her, since they were stranded in the middle of nowhere.

He scanned the screen. "Yep. It's Lincoln, wanting to know why he hasn't heard from me yet."

"Ah. I get it now!" She slapped her hands on her hips. "You pretended to play along with my insanity of venturing out in this weather, all the while reporting me to authorities." Relief swept through her at the realization that Garek hadn't left the safety of the lake house without a backup plan.

He scowled down his nose at her. "So this is the thanks I get for being the man with the plan, eh?"

"Actually, I'm this close," she pinched her thumb and forefinger and held them up in front of him, "to dissolving into tears of gratitude and kissing your snow boots."

"Hold that thought." He pulled up a locater map on his phone and used it to pinpoint their location. Then he sent a screen shot of it with his return message.

"This means he knows exactly where we're at, right?"

"As soon as he receives the coordinates of our location, yes."

"Excellent! Maybe he can send us a few snow-mobiles or something." Her heartbeat quickened in anticipation. It looked as if their failed venture would soon be over.

Lincoln's response was a long one. Garek scanned it, frowning. "Actually, I think he's hoping for a favor in return from us before sending his rescue squad out in this mess."

"Tit for tat, huh?" She wasn't sure how much they had to offer right now, with a stranded hiker out there somewhere and the fact they were huddling two snaps away from the next avalanche themselves.

"Not exactly. Looks like our missing Number Five managed to ping a final message to her twin sister before she settled into radio silence. Her sister called 911, and they routed her call to none other than the Heart Lake Police Department."

"Omigosh! They found her!" Reese clapped her hands in a burst of joy.

"Her call to her sister came through more than

two hours ago. They think they've found where she was at that point in time."

Lincoln's next message flashed across Garek's screen. It was followed by another map — not theirs.

"He said she was right...here." He zoomed in on Lincoln's map. "She fell and landed on some ledge that he thinks may be near our current location." He zoomed out and back in a few times to examine a few other areas on the map. "This looks like an outcropping of rocks, and this..." he pointed, "may be some sort of building."

Reese squinted at it. "It's small."

"Looks like."

"It could be a cabin then." Excitement infused her voice. "This cabin!"

"Let's hope." He leaped to his feet and started donning his snow gear. "If it is, I think I know exactly which direction to head to find Harper Croft."

Reese had to use the arm of an overstuffed plaid chair to stand. "I'm going with you."

"Over my dead body." Garek pointed at the rug she'd just vacated. "A blizzard is no place to be dragging a sprained ankle."

"We don't know for sure that it's sprained." She wrinkled her nose at him. "It might only be bruised."

"Or it could be fractured." His jaw tightened. "I'm sorry, Reese, but you're going to have to sit this one out."

She was only half-listening as she hobbled around the cabin, opening cabinets and rifling through drawers.

"What are you looking for?" He tugged on his boots and zipped up his ski coat.

"A rope long enough to tether you to me."

"Darling—"

She held up a hand. "Don't bother pooh-poohing my latest suggestion, because I'm not listening."

He chuckled. "Un-wad your thermal britches, lady. I was only going to say that it's a great idea."

"Sure you were." She snickered as she continued to yank open cabinet drawers.

A light tap on her shoulder made her spin around. Garek was standing there, arms folded, with an enormous coil of rope hanging off one shoulder. "Is this what you're looking for?"

"Yes! Gimme." She lunged for the rope. "Where did you find it?"

"Come and get it, darling." He caught her in his arms and spun her around, lifting her feet from the floor.

She threw her arms around his neck and held on. "Seriously! Where did you find it?"

"In the pantry. Where else?"

She rolled her eyes. "Yeah, that's the first place anyone would look for a coil of rope."

"It's true. That's where I found it."

"That's kinda creepy. Makes you wonder what kind of person lives here."

"A genius, if you ask me." He set her very carefully back on her feet. "Lucky for us, he turned his pantry into a storage closet. You ought to see all the stuff he has stashed in there — climbing gear, lanterns, flares, you name it."

"Let's just hope it's long enough to get you to Harper Croft's location," Reese sighed, uncoiling the rope. She secured one end of it around his middle. "We still have no idea what condition she's in. Poor thing! You better go prepared for anything and everything."

"Hey, I've got this." Garek pressed a quick kiss to her lips. "Lucky for me, the owner of an award-winning survivalist show helped stock my backpack."

She forced a smile, though her stress level was ratcheting to frantic heights at the thought of him venturing out alone in the storm. "She sounds like an amazing gal. Be sure to thank her for me — *after* you make it safely back with our missing hiker."

He glanced at his cell phone again before pocketing it.

"How's the battery holding out?" Though they hadn't spent much time on their phones, she knew the charge would only last so long.

"The battery's fine," he assured. "It's the reception I'm worried about. It keeps flickering down to one and two bars."

She nodded tightly. "Probably the storm interfering with the service." She gave her end of the rope a gentle shake. "Another good reason not to wander any further than this will take you. We can't afford to get separated."

"Agreed." He palmed her face and gazed deeply into her eyes. "I'll be back in, say, thirty minutes. If you need me sooner, just give the rope a good tug."

"Okay." She had no idea how he was going to keep track of the time if his phone died, but she would try not to worry about that until she had to.

As he opened the door, a cold wind blew in a swirl of snow. It quickly melted from the heat of the fire, leaving tiny puddles of water around the door mat.

Reese hobbled back to the kitchenette in search of a towel to wipe up the dampness. It hurt her ankle to keep putting pressure on it, but she couldn't bring herself to sit back down — not with Garek out there risking the elements to go after their missing contestant.

Breathing a prayer for the woman's safety, Reese hopped to the window and tried to peer out. It was pointless. The snow had formed a solid sheet of whiteness against the glass pane. Out of sheer frustration, she flopped back down on the rug in front of the fire and started text-spamming Lincoln.

She typed the time of day that Garek had left the cabin and informed him that she was holding the other end of the rope he was attached to.

Lincoln's response was lightning quick. *Sorry you're stranded, but I did try to warn you.*

She shot him a heated response. *Hey, I don't report to you, remember?*

He dished it right back. *If you did, you wouldn't be nursing a sprained ankle right now.*

Her lips twitched. Gosh, Garek had really done a thorough job of being a tattle-tale! *Whatevs. Sounds like we're right where you need us to be, officer. Doing a solid for your team...*

He sent her a graphic of a swordsman getting tagged by his fencing partner. *Touché.*

She kept typing. *We were hoping for a little help from you all. Hint hint...*

I'm on it. She could sense his frustration in his response. *The soonest I can safely deploy any mode of transportation, I will.*

Meaning she and Garek could still be stuck out here in the mountains for hours, or even days. Desperate for something to do to keep her mind from conjuring up the worst scenarios, she returned to hobbling around the cabin. There were enough supplies to last two or three trespassers a few days — at least in terms of canned goods and bottled water. However, the stack of firewood was quickly dwindling. That would need to be replenished soon.

Reese cast anxious glances at her cell phone as the minutes ticked by. Ten minutes quickly bled into twenty minutes, then thirty minutes. At the forty-minute mark, she cracked open the front door of the cabin and gave the rope a tug. She waited another ten minutes, and nothing happened.

"Oh, Garek," she muttered feverishly. "Where are you?" She tugged on the rope again. At the one-hour mark, however, there was still no sign of him.

"That's it!" she snapped out loud to the empty cabin. "We had an agreement. You broke your end of it, so now I'm fully justified in breaking mine."

She swiftly donned her snow gear and snatched up her backpack. A sudden inspiration gave her pause. She limped to the pantry storage closet and added a few more supplies to her backpack — two handfuls of the flares, an extra flashlight, a long-neck butane lighter, a whole box of granola bars, and a half dozen more water bottles.

The added weight was noticeable, but she wouldn't be gone long. Before leaving the shelter of the cabin porch, she knotted, re-knotted, then triple-knotted her end of the rope to one of the porch columns. Then she fisted one gloved hand around it. Using it as her guide, she stumbled into the wailing storm.

Mercy! It was bad outside. To avoid the slap of damp snow on her bare skin, she yanked the cords of her hood to pull it mostly closed over her face. It wasn't easy walking on an injured ankle, either. She wished she had the forethought to take a pain pill before leaving the cabin. However, the sharp ache in her ankle ended up having an unexpected side benefit — keeping her alert. At least it did before the numbness of cold set it.

Oh, my lands! I have to find Garek. Soon! Before we all freeze to death out here. There was no way to track the time without subjecting her cell phone to the elements, so Reese moved doggedly forward. After what seemed like an eternity, she reached the other end of the rope.

That's when the chill in the air finally clawed its way through her coat and found its way to her chest. *Oh, Garek! What have you done?* She ran her gloved fingers over the knot he'd made to anchor it to a tree branch. *Where did you go?*

She opened the ties of her hood a few inches. "Garek!" she shouted into the wind. "Where are you?" She mentally ran over the supplies in her back-pack, wondering what she could take out and tie together to extend the area of her search. She had three or four silver mylar blankets. Tied end-to-end, however, they wouldn't stretch far — no more than another twenty feet or so.

"Garek!" she shouted again at the top of her lungs. "Garek?"

The outline of something large lumbered into view.

For a moment, her heart froze, fearing it was a wild animal. *Great. I came all the way out here just to get eaten by a hungry bear.*

She gave a muffled yelp as the creature continued his advance. Twisting around, she struggled to unzip her backpack. Maybe if she could unearth one of the flares, she could use it to scare him off.

As he drew closer, he reached for her.

She flapped her hands frenziedly. "Get back, you crazy—"

"Reese?"

Miracle of miracles! It wasn't a bear after all. It was Garek! "What are you doing out here?" he demanded.

It was too hard to be heard above the howl of the storm, so she saved her breath as he tugged her away from the safety of the tree. They stumbled together over a short, curved mountain path into a darkened cavern.

"Come on," Garek urged, when she started to slide to the ground. "We gotta keep going."

He led her deeper into the cavern along the uneven walkway until the fiercest winds could no longer reach them. Eventually, the path led to a much wider room where a small fire burned. The limp frame of a woman was stretched out beside it.

"So this is where you've been. Is this, ah...?" Reese dropped to the floor to take the weight off of her screaming ankle. She crawled the rest of the way to the woman's side.

"Yes. It's Harper. She's alive." Garek sounded grim. "She's been unconscious ever since I carried her off the ledge, though. Didn't think it was wise to try to cart her all the way back to the cabin. Hopefully, Lincoln and his team will be on their way soon."

"Hopefully." Reese wasn't counting on it, though. Lincoln was right. Until it was safe to deploy reinforcements, he was only risking more lives if he sent anyone else up the mountain — which he didn't seem inclined to do.

Looked like it was going to be solely up to her and Garek to keep Contestant Number Five alive. Reese slid off her gloves and reached for the woman's forehead. Though her own hands felt like ice, the woman's skin wasn't much warmer. She looked like a wilted mermaid beneath her snow gear. Her hair was wound into thick corn row braids, but the melting frost was causing rivulets of water to run down her temples. Freckles stood out in raised relief against her pale cheeks, and her skin was puckered with goosebumps.

"Blankets," Reese muttered. "She needs more blankets." Unfortunately, her hands were so cold, it was difficult to unlatch her backpack.

Garek moved behind her to lift it from her shoulders. "What did you pack? Boulders?"

She shot him a rueful look. "Everything I could possibly squeeze into it."

"You're the perfect woman to be marooned in a snowstorm with." His voice was thick with affection.

"I'm the perfect woman for you. Period."

"No argument there."

"I know everyone else thinks I'm crazy for dragging you out in this storm," she continued, "but I'm glad we did it — sprained ankle and all. I truly believe this is where we were meant to be today. Right here on the side of this mountain."

"Sure looks that way, darling."

"You probably saved this woman's life, Garek."

"We," he corrected. "We saved her life. I wouldn't be in Heart Lake if it wasn't for you, much less out here on this God-forsaken—"

"Now, now!" Reese chuckled.

They worked together to rip open four more packages of blankets and roll them around the ill woman.

"S-so cold," Harper Croft muttered. Her long, reddish brown eyelashes fluttered against her pasty white cheeks.

"Hey, Harper," Reese called softly. "Can you hear me?"

The woman groaned and tried to sit up. "Wh-where am I?"

"On the side of a mountain with two friends. We're here to help you get back to your hotel room."

The woman's eyelids shot open, revealing a startling pair of green eyes. She stared for a moment. "Holy Moly! You're the—"

"Owner of Max West Adventures, yes," Reese supplied flatly. "What were you thinking coming out here alone?" Now that the woman was awake and looking like she was going to recover, Reese's indignation returned to full throttle. The woman had taken a foolish and unnecessary risk.

Harper threw an arm weakly over her eyes. "How did you find me?"

"Your sister called 911 after receiving your last text. The operator managed to put her through to the Heart Lake Police Department."

Harper moved her arm away from her eyes and cracked her eyelids open. "Hadley is probably worried sick about me," she moaned. "As if she didn't have enough already on her plate."

"She'll be thrilled to hear you're okay."

"I'm not okay." The disgruntled contestant struggled to sit up and finally succeeded. "Thanks to that storm blowing out of nowhere, I feel about as strong as a spaghetti noodle. I don't know if I'll recover in time to compete, and we needed that money so badly."

"So we heard." As Reese and Garek exchanged a

sympathetic look, Reese uncapped a water bottle and pressed it into the woman's hands.

"It sounds like my sister told the police everything." Harper's voice shook as she lifted the bottle to her lips.

"Her main concern was finding you," Reese reminded gently.

"Speaking of the police, where are they?" Harper's head swiveled in confusion.

"On their way." *I hope.* Reese infused as much confidence as she could in her answer. "In the meantime, you have us to keep you company."

Harper squinted at the cavern walls. "Do you really think they'll find us here?"

"I do." Garek pulled out his cell phone. "How about we squeeze in an impromptu interview to pass the time while we wait?"

"You want to interview me? I don't even know if I'll still be competing." Harper set the water bottle on the ground beside her, looking weary enough to topple over.

"Just humor me," Garek coaxed.

Reese stared at him, wondering what he was up to. Harper was right. She might not make it to the starting line at this point.

Garek launched into a few open-ended questions about why Harper had wanted to be on the Max West Adventures show in the first place.

She grew teary-eyed as she described her twin sister's rare form of cancer. "We used to do all this kind of stuff together," she informed them with a sniffle. "Bike races, triathlons, skiing competitions...and we loved every minute of it. It breaks my heart to be here in Heart Lake without her, but she needs me to keep being strong for her. To keep competing and to keep winning. Her very life may depend on it." At Garek's prodding, Harper briefly outlined the overseas treatments her sister hoped to receive by Christmas.

"And there you have it." With the push of a button, Garek flipped the camera lens back to him. "Contestant Number Five's very worthy reason for her race to the top. Be sure to tune in for our next update..."

The wail of a distant siren made him break off whatever else he was about to say. "They're here!" He pocketed his phone and jogged toward the opening of the cavern. "They found us!"

Seconds later, Lincoln Hudson, Shep Whitaker and their dogs burst onto the scene. The Golden Retriever and German Shepherds surrounded the trio in the cavern, barking in triumph.

Reese struggled to her feet to place her hand in Garek's as Shep's bemused gaze swept over them.

Instead of the criticism she was expecting, he noted in a quiet voice, "You did it, my slightly insane friend. You really did it. You saved this woman's life."

His dark gaze sharpened with interest as it landed on Harper Croft.

"We did it," Reese corrected softly, awash with the warmth of knowing she and Garek had worked in tandem the entire time. She couldn't have done it without him, nor did she want to. He was the missing piece of her heart, her best friend, and the man she would love until the end of her days.

EPILOGUE

One Day Later

The impromptu blizzard transformed Heart Lake into a winter wonderland just in time for Christmas Eve. Every street and building was drenched in white, making it look as if Reese and her crew were walking around in a postcard. Christmas lights twinkled from the eaves of nearly every home around the lake.

It was the first day of their Max West Adventures winter season, and it looked as if everything was in place to start on time. The arena was jam-packed with locals waiting to cheer on the contestants, who were taking their places on the starting line.

"Get a load of this!" Matt McGraw jogged Reese's way. Instead of taking the steps, he scaled the side of the grandstand and leaned over the silver railing to wave his cell phone at her.

"What's going on?" Reese glanced curiously at his phone.

"We posted Garek's interview with Contestant Number Five on all of our corporate social media sites last night." He beckoned her to take a closer look. "And it's going viral, baby! Look at these views. We're getting hundreds of hits every minute."

"That's not all we're getting." Garek strode up the steps to the grandstand, brandishing his iPad. "The donations are pouring in, too."

"Donations?" Reese reached for his iPad. "Let me see that."

He was right. Their donation button was being flooded with submissions, and their company account balance was spiking to new heights. "All of this happened because of one short interview?"

"Yep. Looks like Harper's story has stirred a flurry of Christmas spirit. More than half of these donations are for her sister's cancer treatments."

"Are you serious?" Reese stared at Garek in amazement.

"It's a Christmas miracle!" Matt crowed. Leaping down from the railing, he made a rally sign with one finger. "Well, I'm off to check everyone's gear and supplies one last time."

"Speaking of miracles." Garek sidled closer to Reese. Sliding his arm around her shoulders, he angled his head at the starting line. "Look who showed up."

Though she still looked a little pale from her blizzard escapade, Harper Croft was taking her place. Shep Whitaker made a beeline for her in his ridiculous chicken costume. They watched as he bent to adjust a strap on the woman's skis. Then he reached up to tweak something on her hat.

"That's awfully nice of him to extend so much kindness to a fellow contestant," Reese murmured in a voice brimming with humor.

"I was thinking the same thing," he retorted dryly. "I'm sure it has nothing to do with the fact that she resembles a fairytale princess."

"Fairytale material, huh?" Reese glanced laughingly up at him. "Should I be jealous?"

"Not even a little." He bent his head to plant a lingering kiss on her lips in full view of their audience. "I'm just hoping it means Chicken Boy has finally given up his aspirations in your direction."

"Aw, are you afraid of a little competition?" she teased.

"Heck, yeah. He's a cop with a badge and a chicken suit, and I'm just a lowly, featherless camera man."

"I think you mean business partner." She slid an arm around his middle and gave him a squeeze hug. "I sent an email to my attorney last night to see what it'll take to finally make our partnership official."

"Is that so, darling?"

"It's so, my featherless camera guy." She gave him another hug. "In case you're wondering, I much prefer you without feathers."

"I wasn't wondering about that, actually, though I do like where you're going with the partnership thing."

"Me, too," she sighed happily, tipping her head against his shoulder. "I can't wait until it's officially official."

At his silence, she murmured, "This is what you want, too, right?" She hoped she hadn't misread any cues and jumped to the wrong conclusion.

"Actually, I had a different kind of partnership in mind." Garek brushed a kiss against the top of her head. Then he reached for her hands and slowly took a knee in front of her.

A collective gasp rose from the stands as their onlookers perceived what was happening.

Reese gazed down at him in wonder. "Garek," she breathed. "What are you—?"

"Will you marry me, Reese?" All the hope and joy of the holidays was reflected in his eyes. "I want to be more than best friends and business partners. I want to be all yours, now and forever."

Tears glinted off her lashes as she nodded. "Yes," she choked. "I want that, too."

She distantly perceived Matt jogging their way,

camera rolling. "It's another Christmas miracle," he shouted.

Garek produced a white-gold ring with a square diamond that glittered in the sunlight as if powered by tiny Christmas lights. He slid it on her finger, then stood to take her in his arms again.

"She said yes!" someone cried. The crowd erupted into clapping and cheering.

Reese's heart was overflowing as Garek claimed her lips in a tender kiss brimming with a thousand more unspoken promises. As she returned his kiss, a sudden thought made her heart skip a beat. Her mother had been right about them. She'd known they were in love long before her only daughter had realized it.

Reese twined her arms around Garek's neck. "I love you so much!"

"I love you, too, darling." He reached behind his neck to take one of her hands in his.

She was surprised to feel the metallic grip of a pop gun.

They raised their joined hands, clutching the gun between them.

"Ten, nine, eight, seven!" Their audience roared out the countdown to the starting time.

"Six, five, four, three, two, one!" Garek's finger pressed hers into the trigger. The gun went off, sending a white plume of smoke into the air.

Reese and Garek watched in pride as all twelve

of their contestants skied from the arena. She knew deep in her heart that it was more than the beginning of a race. It was the beginning of so much more.

Her bachelorette days were over. Not only had Garek helped rescue their missing hiker, he'd also rescued her heart from a lifetime of loneliness.

I didn't even realize I needed rescuing, but Mom did.

The sun glinted off the snow-capped mountains on the horizon like the wink of an angel. Reese squeezed Garek's hand, thrilled to know that this Christmas marked the beginning of many more Christmases together.

Like this book? Leave a review now!

Ready to read about my next Texas Hotline hero? When a former bodybuilder joins the world of search and rescue operations, and gets to put his skills — and his heart — to the test right away helping a stranded hiker...
Keep turning for a sneak peek at
The Rebound Rescue*!*

Can't get enough of Jo's sweet romance stories on the shores of Heart Lake? Good! Because there's a Santa-sized mystery brewing in the new mayor's office that *may force her to turn to the hunkiest, most sarcastic cowboy in town for help. Check out **Thousands of Gifts**, and be swept away by another swoon-worthy hero this Christmas!*

Much love,
Jo

SNEAK PREVIEW: THE REBOUND RESCUE

An ex-bodybuilder — recovering from a broken heart — throws himself wholeheartedly into search and rescue operations, while a genius research scientist plots to redirect some of his hunky attention to her.

After a bad breakup, former bodybuilding champion Jett Channing decides to go on a girlfriend diet. So when his normal responsibilities as a forest ranger are interrupted to rescue a stranded hiker, he jumps at the chance to work off his wounded pride by doing something so meaningful and worthwhile.

Gwyneth Moore can't believe her T.V. celebrity boyfriend of three years is dumping her for an anemic-looking supermodel. Too crushed to return to her job as a university research scientist, she decides to take the afternoon off to study a rare breed of flowers at the Sam Houston National Park.

When she slips down a steep incline and becomes trapped on a narrow ledge, she is stunned speechless to discover the super-hot Jet Channing is the one who's been sent to her rescue. Maybe it's her dehydration and exposure to the elements taking over, but Gwyneth finds herself crushing on the swoon-worthy ranger who's literally trying to talk her off the ledge in a daring rescue attempt. And it's way too bad he's not looking for a new girlfriend, because that's exactly the vacancy she wants to fill if she survives her fall!

Grab your copy in eBook, paperback, or Kindle Unlimited on Amazon!
The Rebound Rescue

Complete series. Read them all!
The Plus One Rescue
The Secret Baby Rescue
The Bridesmaid Rescue
The Girl Next Door Rescue
The Secret Crush Rescue
The Bachelorette Rescue
The Rebound One Rescue

The Fake Bride Rescue
The Blind Date Rescue
The Maid by Mistake Rescue
The Unlucky Bride Rescue
The Temporary Family Rescue

Much love,
Jo

NOTE FROM JO

Guess what? There's more going on in the lives of the hunky heroes you meet in my stories.

Because...*drum roll*...I have some Bonus Content for

everyone who signs up for my mailing list. From now on, there will be a special bonus content for each new book I write, just for my subscribers. Also, you'll hear about my next new book as soon as it's out (*plus you get a free book in the meantime*). Woohoo!

As always, thank you for reading and loving my books!

JOIN CUPPA JO READERS!

If you're on Facebook, please join my group, Cuppa Jo Readers. Don't miss out on the giveaways + all the sweet and swoony cowboys!

https://www.facebook.com/groups/ CuppaJoReaders

FREE BOOK!

Don't forget to join my mailing list for new releases, freebies, special discounts, and Bonus Content. Plus, you get a FREE sweet romance book for signing up!

https://BookHip.com/JNNHTK

Heart Lake

A *newly elected mayor bubbling with holiday spirit, a sarcastic cowboy determined to put a dent in her optimism, and the charity project that puts him at real risk of falling for the enemy...*

Mayor Heavenly Remington decides that this is the year every child in Heart Lake will receive a Christmas gift, no matter how much budget finagling and additional fundraising it takes. Weary of town officials making promises they can't keep, cowboy farmer Wes Hawling taunts his fellow citizens into flooding her children's charity project with prank requests — each one more absurd than the last.

Instead of giving up like he expects, she doubles down on her efforts to hunt down every gift on the wish lists of her youngest constituents by Christmas Eve. When a threat to the town forces him to become her grudging accomplice for a few days, he is shocked to discover how close she is to meeting her goal. The fact that he finds himself secretly cheering her on might just be the biggest Christmas miracle of all!

Welcome to Heart Lake! A small town teaming with old family rivalries, the rumble of horses' hooves, and folks on both sides of the law and everywhere in between — faith-filled romance that you'll never forget.

Thousands of Gifts
Available in eBook, paperback, and Kindle Unlimited!

Read them all!
Winds of Change
Song of Nightingales
Perils of Starlight
Return of Miracles
Thousands of Gifts
Race of Champions

Storm of Secrets
Season of Angels

Much love,
   Jo

SNEAK PREVIEW: ACCIDENTAL HERO

MATT

I *can't believe I fell for her lies!*

Feeling like the world's biggest fool, Matt Romero gripped the steering wheel of his white Ford F-150. He was cruising up the sunny interstate toward Amarillo, where he had an interview in the morning; but he was arriving a day early to get the lay of the land. Well, that was partly true, anyway. The real reason he couldn't leave Sweetwater, Texas fast enough was because *she* lived there.

It was one thing to be blinded by love. It was another thing entirely to fall for the stupidest line in a cheater's handbook.

Cat sitting. I actually allowed her to talk me into cat sitting! Or house sitting, which was what it actually amounted to by the time he'd collected his fiancée's mail and carried her latest batch of Amazon deliveries inside. All of that was in addition to feeding and watering her cat and scooping out the litter box.

It wasn't that he minded doing a favor now and then for the woman he planned to spend the rest of his life with. What he minded was that she wasn't in New York City doing her latest modeling gig, like she'd claimed. *Nope.* Nowhere near the Big Apple. She'd been shacked up with another guy. In town. Less than ten miles away from where he'd been cat sitting.

To make matters worse, she'd recently talked Matt into leaving the Army — for her. Or *them*, she'd insisted. A bittersweet decision he'd gladly made, so they could spend more quality time together as a couple. So he could give her the attention she wanted and deserved. So they could have a real marriage when the time came.

Unfortunately, by the time he'd finished serving his last few months of duty as an Army Ranger, she'd already found another guy and moved on. She hadn't even had the decency to tell him! If it wasn't for her own cat blowing her cover, heaven only knew when he would've found out about her unfaithfulness. Two days before their wedding, however, on that fateful cat sitting mission, Sugarball had knocked their first-date picture off the coffee table, broken the glass, and revealed the condemning snapshot his bride-to-be had hidden beneath the top photo. One of her and her newest boyfriend.

And now I'm single, jobless, and mad as a—

The scream of sirens jolted Matt back to the present. A glance in his rearview mirror confirmed his suspicions. He was getting pulled over. *For what?* A scowl down at his speedometer revealed he was cruising at no less than 95 mph. *Whoa!* It was a good twenty miles over the posted speed limit. *Okay, this is bad.* He'd be lucky if he didn't lose his license over this — his fault entirely for driving distracted without his cruise control on. *My day just keeps getting better.*

Slowing and pulling his truck to the shoulder, he coasted to a stop and waited. And waited. And waited some more. A peek at his side mirror showed the cop was still sitting in his car and talking on his phone. *Give me a break.*

To ease the ache between his temples, Matt reached for the red cooler he'd propped on the passenger seat and dragged out a can of soda. He popped the tab and tipped it up to chug down a much-needed shot of caffeine. He hadn't slept much the last couple of nights. Sleeping in a hotel bed wasn't all that restful. Nor was staying in a hotel in the same town where his ex lived. His very public figure of an ex, whose super-model figure appeared in all too many commercials, posters, magazine articles, and online gossip rags.

Movement in his rearview mirror caught his attention. He watched as the police officer finally opened his door, unfolded his large frame from the front seat of his black SUV, and stood. But he continued talking on his phone. *Are you kidding me?* Matt swallowed a dry chuckle and took another swig of his soda. It was a good thing he'd hit the road the day before his interview at the Pantex nuclear plant. The way things were going, it might take the rest of the day to collect his speeding ticket.

By his best estimate, he'd reached the outskirts of Amarillo, maybe twenty or thirty miles out from his final destination. He'd already passed the exit signs for Hereford. Or the beef capital of the world, as the small farm town was often called.

He reached across the dashboard to open his glove compartment and fish out his registration card and proof of insurance. There was going to be no talking his way out of this one, unless the officer happened to have a soft spot for soldiers. He seriously doubted any guy in blue worth his spit would have much sympathy for someone going twenty miles over the speed limit, though.

Digging for his wallet, he pulled out his driver's license. Out of sheer habit, he reached inside the slot where he normally kept his military ID and found it empty. *Right.* He no longer possessed one, which left him with an oddly empty feeling.

He took another gulp of soda and watched as the officer finally pocketed his cell phone. *Okay, then. Time to get this party started.* Matt chunked his soda can in the nearest cup holder and stuck his driver's license, truck registration, and insurance card between two fingers. Hitting an automatic button on the door, he lowered his window a few inches and waited.

The guy heading his way wore the uniform of a Texas state trooper — blue tie, tan Stetson pulled low over his eyes, and a bit of a swagger as he strode to stand beside Matt's window.

"License and registration, soldier."

Guess I didn't need my military ID, after all, to prove I'm a soldier. An ex soldier, that is. Matt had all but forgotten about the Ranger tab displayed on his license plate. He wordlessly poked the requested items through the window opening.

"Any reason you're in such a hurry this morning?" the officer mused in a curious voice as he glanced over Matt's identification. He was so tall, he had to stoop to peer through the window. Like Matt, he was tan, brown haired, and sporting a goatee. However, the officer was a good several inches taller.

"Nothing worth hearing, officer." *My problem. Not yours. Don't want to talk about it.* Matt squinted through the glaring sun to read the guy's name on his tag. *McCarty.*

"Yeah, well, we have plenty of time to chat, since this is going to be a hefty ticket to write up." Officer McCarty's tone was mildly sympathetic, though it was impossible to read his expression behind his sunglasses. "I clocked you going twenty-two miles over the posted limit, Mr. Romero."

Twenty-two miles? Not good. Not good at all. Matt's jaw tightened, and he could feel the veins in his temples throbbing. Looked like he was going to have to share his story, after all. Maybe, just maybe, the trooper would feel so sorry for him that he'd give him a warning. It was worth a try, anyway. *If nothing else, it'll give you something to snicker about over your next coffee break.*

"Today was supposed to be my wedding day." He spoke through stiff lips, finding a strange sort of relief in confessing that sorry fact to a perfect stranger. Fortunately, they'd never have to see each other again.

"I'm sorry for your loss." Officer McCarty glanced up from Matt's license to give him what felt like a hard stare. Probably trying to gauge if he was telling the truth or not.

Matt glanced away, wanting to set the man's misconception straight but not wishing to witness his pity when he did. "She's still alive," he muttered. "Found somebody else, that's all." He gripped the steering wheel and drummed his thumbs against it. *I'm just the poor sap she lied to and cheated on heaven only knew how many times.*

He was so done with women, as in never again going to put his heart on the chopping block of love. *Better to live a lonely life than to let another person destroy you like that.* She'd taken everything from him that mattered — his pride, his dignity, and his career.

"Ouch!" Officer McCarty sighed. "Well, here comes the tough part about my job. Despite your reasons, you were shooting down the highway like a bat out of Hades, which was putting lives at risk. Yours, included."

"Can't disagree with that." Matt stared straight ahead, past the small spidery nick in his windshield. He'd gotten hit by a rock earlier while passing a semi tractor trailer. It really hadn't been his day. Or his week. Or his year, for that matter. It didn't mean he was going to grovel, though. The guy might as well give him his ticket and be done with it.

A massive dump truck on the oncoming side of the highway abruptly swerved into the narrow, grassy median. It was a few hundred yards or so away, but his front left tire dipped down, *way* down, and the truck pitched heavily to one side.

"Whoa!" Matt shouted, pointing to get Officer McCarty's attention. "That guy's in trouble!"

Two vehicles on their side of the road passed their parked vehicles in quick succession. A rusted blue van pulling a fifth wheel and a shiny red Dodge Ram. New looking.

Matt laid on his horn to warn them, just as the dump truck started to roll. It was like watching a horror movie in slow motion, knowing something bad was about to happen while being helpless to stop it.

The dump truck slammed onto its side and skidded noisily across Matt's lane. The blue van whipped to the right shoulder in a vain attempt to avoid a collision. Matt winced as the van's bumper caught the hood of the skidding dump truck nearly head on, then jack-knifed into the air like a gigantic inchworm.

The driver of the red truck was only a few car lengths behind, jamming so hard on its brakes that it left two dark smoking lines of rubber on the pavement. Seconds later, it careened into the median and flipped on its side. It wasn't immediately clear if the red pickup had collided with any part of the dump truck. However, an ominous swirl of smoke seeped from its hood.

For a split second, Matt and Officer McCarty stared in shock at each other. Then the officer shoved his license and registration back through the opening in the window. "Suddenly got better things to do than give you a ticket." He sprinted for his SUV, leaped inside, and gunned it around Matt with his sirens blaring and lights flashing. He drove a short distance and stopped with his vehicle canted across both lanes, forming a temporary blockade.

Matt might no longer be in the military, but his protect-and-defend instincts kicked in. There was no telling how long it could take the emergency vehicles to arrive, and he didn't like the way the red pick up was smoking. The driver hadn't climbed out of the cab which wasn't a good sign.

Officer McCarty reached the blue van first, probably because it was the closest, and assisted a dazed man from one of the back passenger doors. He led the guy to the side of the road, helped him get seated on a small incline, then jogged back to help the next passenger exit the van. Unfortunately, Officer McCarty was only one man, and this was much bigger than a one-man job.

Following his gut, Matt flung off his emergency brake and gunned his motor up the shoulder, pausing a few car lengths back from the collision. Turning off his motor, he leaped from his truck and jogged across the double lane to the red pickup. The motor was still running, and the smoke was rising more thickly now.

Holy snap! Whoever was in there needed to get out immediately before it caught fire or exploded. Arriving at the suspended tailgate of the doomed truck, he took a flying leap and nimbly scaled the cab to reach the driver's door. Unsurprisingly, it was locked.

Pounding on the window, Matt shouted at the driver. "You okay in there?"

There was no answer and no movement. Peering closer, he could make out the still form of a woman. Blonde, pale, and curled to one side. The only thing holding her in place was the snarl of a seatbelt around her waist. A trickle of red ran across one cheek.

Matt's survival training kicked in. Crouching over the side of the truck, he quickly assessed the damage to the windshield and decided it wasn't enough to make it the best entry point. *Too bad.* Because his only other option was to shower the driver with glass. *Sorry, lady!* Swinging a leg, he jabbed the back edge of his boot heel into the edge of the glass, nearest the lock. His luck held when he managed to pop a fist-sized hole instead of shattering the entire pane.

Reaching inside, he unlocked the door and pulled it open. The next part was a little trickier, since he had to reach down, *way* down, to unbuckle the woman and catch her weight before she fell. It would've been easier is she was conscious and able to follow instructions. Instead, he was going to have to rely on his many years of physical training.

I can do this. I have to do this. An ominous hiss of steam and smoke from beneath the front hood stiffened his resolve and made him move faster.

"Come on, lady," Matt muttered, releasing her seatbelt and catching her. With a grunt of exertion, he hefted her free of the mangled cab. Then he half-slid, half hopped to the ground with her in his arms and took off at a jog.

Clad in jeans, boots, and a pink and white plaid

shirt, she was lighter than he'd been expecting. Her upper arm, that his left hand was cupped around, felt desperately thin despite her baggy shirt. It was as if she'd recently been ill and lost a lot of weight. One long, strawberry blonde braid dangled over her shoulder, and a sprinkle of freckles stood out in stark relief against her pale cheeks.

He hoped like heck she hadn't hit her head too hard on impact. Visions of various traumatic brain injuries and their various complications swarmed through his mind, along with the possibility he'd just moved a woman with a broken neck. *Please don't be broken.*

Since the road was barricaded, he carried the woman to the far right shoulder and up a grassy knoll where Officer McCarty was depositing the other injured victims. A dry wind gusted, sending a layer of fine-grain dust in their direction, along with one prickly, rolling tumbleweed. About twenty yards away was a rocky canyon wall that went straight up, underscoring the fact that there really hadn't been any way for the hapless van and pickup drivers to avoid the collision. They'd literally been trapped between the canyon and oncoming traffic.

An explosion ricocheted through the air. Matt's back was turned to the mangled pile of vehicles, but the blast shook the ground beneath him. On pure instinct, he dove for the grass, using his body as a shield over the woman in his arms. He used one hand to cradle her head against his chest and his other to break their fall as best as he could.

A few people cried out in fear, as smoke billowed around them, blanketing the scene. For the next few minutes, it was difficult to see much, and the wave of ensuing heat had a suffocating feel to it. The woman beneath Matt remained motionless, though he was pretty sure she mumbled something a few times. He crouched over her, keeping her head cradled beneath his hand. A quick exam determined she was breathing normally, but she was still unconscious. He debated what to do next.

The howl of a fire engine sounded in the distance. His shoulders slumped in relief. Help had finally arrived. More sirens blared, and the area was soon crawling with fire engines, ambulances, and paramedics with stretchers. One walked determinedly in his direction through the dissipating smoke.

"What's your name, sir?" the EMT worker inquired in calm, even tones. Her chin-length dark hair was blowing nearly sideways in the wind. She shook her head to knock it away, revealing a pair of snapping dark eyes that were full of concern.

"I'm Sergeant Matt Romero," he informed her out of sheer habit. *Well, maybe no longer the sergeant part.* "I'm fine. This woman is not. I don't know her name. She was unconscious when I pulled her from her truck."

As the curvy EMT stepped closer, Matt could read her name tag. *Corrigan.* "I'm Star Corrigan, and I'll do whatever I can to help." Her forehead wrinkled in alarm as she caught sight of the injured woman's face. "Omigosh! Bree?" Tossing her red medical bag on the ground, she slid to her knees beside them. "Oh, Bree, honey!" she sighed, reaching for her pulse.

"I-I..." The woman stirred. Her lashes fluttered a few times against her cheeks. Then they snapped open, revealing two pools of the deepest blue Matt had ever seen. They held a very glazed-over look in them as they latched onto his face. "Don't go," she pleaded with a hitch to her voice that might've been due to emotion or the amount of smoke she'd inhaled.

Either way, it tugged at every one of his heartstrings. There was a lost ring to her voice, along with an air of distinct vulnerability, that made him want to take her in his arms again and cuddle her close.

"I won't," he promised huskily, hardly knowing what he was saying. He probably would have said anything to make the desperate look in her eyes go away.

"I'm not loving her heart rate." Star produced a penlight and flipped it on. Shining it in one of her friend's eyes, then the other, she cried urgently, "Bree? It's me, Star Corrigan. Can you tell me what happened, hon?"

A shiver worked its way through Bree's too-thin frame. "Don't go," she whispered again to Matt, before her eyelids fluttered closed. Another shiver worked its way through her, despite the fact she was no longer conscious.

"She's going into shock." Star glanced worriedly over her shoulder. "Need a stretcher over here!" she called sharply. One was swiftly rolled their way.

Matt helped her lift and deposit their precious burden aboard.

"Can you make it to the hospital?" Star asked as he helped push the stretcher toward the nearest ambulance. "Bree seemed pretty intent on having you stay with her."

Matt's brows shot up in surprise. "Uh, sure." As far as he could tell, he'd never laid eyes on the injured woman before today. More than likely she'd mistaken him for someone else. He didn't mind helping out, though. *Who knows?* Maybe he could give her medical team some information about the rescue that they might find useful in her treatment.

Or maybe he was just drawn to the fragile-looking Bree for reasons he couldn't explain. What-ever the case, he found he wasn't in a terrible hurry to bug out of there. He had plenty of extra time built into his schedule before his interview tomorrow. The only real task he had left for the day was finding a hotel room once he reached Amarillo.

"I just need to let Officer McCarty know I'm

leaving." Matt shook his head sheepishly. "I kinda hate to admit this, but he had me pulled over for speeding when this all went down." He waved a hand at the carnage around them. It was a dismal sight of twisted, blackened metal and scorched pavement. All three vehicles were totaled.

Star snickered, then seemed to catch herself. "Sorry. Inappropriate laughter. Very inappropriate laughter."

He shrugged, not in the least offended. A lot of people laughed when they were nervous or upset, which she clearly was about her unconscious friend. "Guess it was pretty stupid of me to be driving these long empty stretches without my cruise control on." Especially with the way he'd been seething and brooding nearly non-stop for the past seventy-two hours.

Star shot him a sympathetic look. "Believe me, I'm not judging. Far from it." She reached out to pat Officer McCarty's arm as they passed him with the stretcher. "The only reason a bunch of us in Hereford don't have a lot more points on our licenses, is because we grew up with this sweet guy."

"Aw, shoot! Is that Bree?" Officer McCarty groaned. He pulled his sunglasses down to take a closer look over the top of them. His stoic expression was gone. In its place was one etched with worry. The personal kind. Like Star, he knew the victim.

"Yeah." Star's pink glossy lips twisted. "She and her brother can't catch a break, can they?"

Since they were only a few feet from the back of an ambulance and since two more paramedics converged on them to help lift the stretcher, Matt peeled away to face the trooper who'd pulled him over.

"Any issues with me following them to the hospital, officer? Star asked if I would." Unfortunately, it would give the guy more time and opportunity to ticket Matt, but that couldn't be helped.

"Emmitt," Officer McCarty corrected. "Just call me Emmitt, alright? I think you more than worked off your ticket back there."

"Thanks, man. Really appreciate it." Matt held out a hand, relieved to hear he'd be keeping his license.

They soberly shook hands, eyeing each other.

"You need me to come by the PD to file a witness report or anything before I boogie out of town?"

"Nah. Just give me a call, and we'll take care of it over the phone." Emmitt pulled out his wallet and produced a business card. "Not sure if we'll need your story, since I saw how it went down, but we should probably still cross every T."

"Roger that." Matt stuffed the card in the back pocket of his jeans.

"Where are you headed, anyway?"

"Amarillo. Got an interview at Pantex tomorrow."

"Solid company." Emmitt nodded. "Got several friends who work up there."

Star leaned out from the back of the ambulance. "You coming?" she called to Matt.

He nodded vigorously and jogged toward his truck. Since the ambulance was on the opposite side of the accident, he turned on his blinker, crossed the lanes near Emmitt's SUV, and put his oversized tires to good use traversing the pitchy median. He had to spin his wheels a bit in the center of the median to get his tires to grab the sandy incline leading to the other side of the highway. Once past the accident, he had to re-cross the median to get back en route. It was a good thing he'd upgraded his truck for off-roading purposes.

They continued north and drove the final twenty minutes or so to Amarillo, which boasted a much bigger hospital than any of the smaller surrounding towns. Luckily, Matt was able to grab a decently close parking spot just as another vehicle was leaving. He jogged into the waiting room, dropped Star Corrigan's name a few times, and tried to make it sound like he was a close friend of the patient. A "close friend" who sadly didn't even know her last name.

The receptionist made him wait while she paged Star, who appeared a short time later to escort him back. "She's in Bay 6," she informed him in a strained voice, reaching for his arm and practically dragging him behind the curtain.

If anything, Bree looked even thinner and more fragile than she had outside on the highway. A nurse was bent over her, inserting an I.V.

"She still hasn't woken up. Hasn't even twitched." Star's voice was soft, barely above a whisper. "They're pretty sure she has a concussion. Gonna run the full battery of tests to figure out what's going on for sure."

Matt nodded, not knowing what to say.

The EMT's pager went off. She snatched it up and scowled at it. "Just got another call. It's a busy day out there for motorists." She punched in a reply, then cast him a sideways glance. "Any chance you can stick around until Bree's brother gets here?"

That's when it hit him that this had been her real goal all along — to ensure that her friend wasn't left alone. She'd known she could get called away to the next job at any second.

"No problem." He offered what he hoped was a reassuring smile. Amarillo was his final destination, anyway. "This is where I was headed, actually. Got an interview at Pantex in the morning."

"No kidding! Well, good luck with that," she returned with a curious, searching look. "A lot of my friends moved up this way for jobs after high school."

Emmitt had said the same thing. "Hey, ah..." He

hated detaining her a second longer than necessary, since she was probably heading out to handle another emergency. However, it might not hurt to know a few more details about the unconscious Bree if he was to be left alone with her. "Mind telling me Bree's last name?"

"Anderson. Her bother is Brody. Brody Anderson. They run a ranch about halfway between here and Hereford, so it'll take him a good twenty minutes or so to get here."

"No problem. I can stay. It was nice meeting you, by the way." His gaze landed on Bree's left hand, which was resting limply atop the white blankets on her bed. It was bare of a wedding ring. *Why did I look? I'm a complete idiot for looking.* He forced his gaze back to the EMT. "Sorry about the circumstances, though."

"Me, too." She shot another worried look at her friend and dropped her voice conspiratorially. "Hey, you're really not supposed to be back here since you're not family, but I sorta begged and they sorta agreed to fudge on the rules until Brody gets here." She eyed him worriedly.

"Don't worry." He could tell she hated the necessity of leaving. "I'll stay until he gets here, even if I get booted out to the waiting room with the regular Joes."

"Thanks! Really." She whipped out her cell

phone. "Here's my number in case you need to reach me for anything."

Well, that was certainly a smooth way to work a pickup line into the conversation. Not that Matt was complaining. His sorely depleted ego could use the boost. He dug for his phone. "Ready."

She rattled off her number, and he quickly texted her back so she would have his.

"Take care of her for me, will you, Matt?" she pleaded anxiously.

On second thought, that was real worry in her voice without any trace of a come-on. Maybe Star hadn't been angling for his number, after all. Maybe she was just that desperate to ensure her friend wasn't going to be left alone in the ER. He nodded his agreement and fist-bumped her.

She tapped back, pushed past the curtain, and was gone. The nurse followed, presumably to report Bree's vitals to the ER doctor on duty.

Matt moved to the foot of the hospital bed. "So who do you think I am, Bree?" *Why did you ask me to stay?*

Her long blonde lashes remained resting against her cheeks. It looked like he was going to have to stick around for a while if he wanted answers.

I hope you enjoyed the first chapter of

BORN IN TEXAS #1: Accidental Hero.
Available in eBook, paperback, and Kindle Unlimited!

Read them all!
A - Accidental Hero
B - Best Friend Hero
C - Celebrity Hero
D - Damaged Hero
E - Enemies to Hero
F - Forbidden Hero
G - Guardian Hero
H - Hunk and Hero
I - Instantly Her Hero
J - Jilted Hero
K - Kissable Hero

Much love,
Jo

For the most up-to-date printable list of my books:

Click here

or go to:

https://www.JoGrafford.com/books

For the most up-to-date printable list of books by Jo Grafford, writing as Jovie Grace (*sweet historical romance*):

Click here

or go to:

https://www.jografford.com/joviegracebooks

ABOUT JO

Jo is an Amazon bestselling author of sweet and inspirational romance stories about faith, hope, love and family drama with a few Texas-sized detours into comedy. She also writes sweet and inspirational historical romance as Jovie Grace.

1.) Follow on Amazon!
amazon.com/author/jografford

2.) Join Cuppa Jo Readers!
https://www.facebook.com/groups/
CuppaJoReaders

3.) Follow on Bookbub!

https://www.bookbub.com/authors/jo-grafford

4.) Follow on Instagram!
https://www.instagram.com/jografford/

5.) Follow on YouTube
https://www.youtube.com/channel/
UC3R1at97Qso6BXiBIxCjQ5w

amazon.com/authors/jo-grafford

bookbub.com/authors/jo-grafford

facebook.com/jografford

instagram.com/jografford

pinterest.com/jografford

Made in the USA
Monee, IL
28 January 2023

26618673R10114